I0712937

THE WOLF EXPERIMENT

Laura Daleo

The Wolf Experiment is a work of fiction. Names, characters, places, and incidents either are the product of the author's imagination or are used fictitiously. Any resemblance to actual persons, living or dead, events, or locales is entirely coincidental.

Copyright © 2026 by Laura Daleo

All rights reserved

Published in the United States by Author Laura Daleo, Tucson, Arizona

Print ISBN: 978-1-7366103-6-7

ebook ISBN: 978-1-7366103-7-4

ALSO BY LAURA DALEO

Immortal Kiss

Bound by Blood

The Vampire Within

The Vow

The Soul Collector

The Doll

Once We Were Witches

My Name Is Death

Book Review by Roger

"The Wolf Experiment by Laura Daleo is a Paranormal Fantasy that blew me away, capturing the imagination of a fantasy and the phenomena of a paranormal thriller. The book takes place in a small town of Doford Peaks, a town nestled in a mountainous region of the country. The book's MMC is Ethan, a nineteen-year-old with a chronic breathing disorder, who prefers his two wolves, Gracie and Hank, over humans companionship. Ethan lives with his grandmother, who happens to be the town's doctor and surgeon. Ethan's parents are also doctors, but he hasn't seen them in fourteen years. They are on a mission to find the cure for Ethan's illness. While on a walk one day with his grandmother, the two wolves pick up a scent and lead the pair to a cave. The wolves rush into the cave, with Ethan and his grandmother following, and find an unconscious, wounded, and seriously dehydrated young woman, wearing a hospital gown, whom they save. They find out the girl's name is Mia, but little else. As Mia is healing, she and Ethan begin to feel a connection, and it grows stronger with each day. When a strange event occurs involving Mia, her story begins to unravel, and Ethan learns that Mia is involved in a clandestine, black-ops government operation that could put everyone in deadly jeopardy.

Laura Daleo does a fabulous job of constructing a thrilling, thoughtful, and dramatic paranormal story. The story is highly emotional in many aspects, especially the relationship between Ethan and Mia. The plot was cleverly written from dark and ominous to sweet and romantic, and the pages seem to turn themselves. The pacing is steady, and the action is incredible, with heart-pounding excitement to keep the reader wanting more. This is a book that is hard to put down and is guaranteed to satisfy the itch that most paranormal thriller readers are seeking."

Book Review by Beba

"This story starts off innocently enough, a young man, on the verge of adulthood, finds a young girl in the dead of winter, in a cave, unconscious. Nursed back to heath, a beautiful friendship turns into a beautiful romance. Then the smooth gears screech grindingly to a halt, and what follows, turns into one so full of anguish, of darkness, and, at times, horrifying, woven expertly into the fabric of the tale. A chance encounter with a high school bully, changed the entire tone of the read, that had me so agog, I was afraid to blink in case I missed something. A truth was revealed, exposing a clandestine black ops and a scary, very daring plan of action is initiated. Which, as plans go, was not so simple, spiking my adrenaline big time!

I'll start at the beginning…Abandoned by his parents at the age of five, handed over to his grandmother, as though he were a disposable commodity, it's no wonder Ethan is an introvert and a loner. Add to that, he's asthmatic and you get an insight into him right off the bat. And I loved him immediately. His two best friends are his wolves, yes, wolves he'd saved as pups, who are just as opinionated and needy as your average dog. And the love they have and shower on Ethan is obvious. He has the most awesome grandma, Evelyn, a doctor, is supportive, loving, if a bit overprotective, which is understandable with his condition. She believes in him, believes he has all the tools, he just needs to be careful,

"Sometimes being brave means understanding your limits". Finding Mia in the cave seemed per chance but it was far from that.

Filthy, wounded, unconscious Mia recovers quickly from her ordeal, but claims insomnia because the truth is horrific. Loved her. She is wounded in more ways than just physical, she's psychologically wounded, she's emotionally wounded and Ethan is her lifeline. Desperate to lead a normal life, so when her truth surfaces, and an opportunity arises to end the covert agency, she jumps in immediately. But...yes .. it's complicated. Ethan and Evelyn are right and centre involved, not personally, and both are shocked at the revelations. Although Mia, Ethan and Evelyn were the main focus, Ms Daleo brought in a whole host of great characters, like Sheriff Reid, Briggs and Locke, and not to forget the coolest wolves, Gracie and Hank.

I do enjoy this author's style of writing, vivid, descriptive, it's fast paced, charged with emotion, awesome action, a mystery or two, and deliciously dark. By no means a light read, this author captures the reality of bullying, of the desperation one with asthma feels when they can't breathe. The HEA hits the right spot, after all the trauma, a warmth settles, not only in Mia and Ethan, but in me too."

CHAPTER 1

A whimper pulled me from my sleep, and my eyelids fluttered open. Gracie's snout was right in front of me, her light gray fur softly brushing against my cheek. As her pale blue eyes looked into mine, her tail began to wag. There was no way I was getting up, and I rolled over to the other side of my bed, where Hank stood waiting. He fixed his golden eyes on me, his pure white fur seeming darker in the dim light of my bedroom. Sunlight filtered through the two large skylights above my bed, casting a warm light over my room. The rays continued to spread across posters of my favorite bands, my world map marked with where I wanted to visit, my only plant that I hadn't killed, and my high school guitar leaning against my bookcase. My wolves whimpered again, signaling it was time to get up. Glancing at the clock on my nightstand, it read 6:00 a.m.

I pulled the covers over my head and tried to fall back asleep, but that didn't work out well. My wolves howled as they jumped onto my king-sized bed. Sitting up, I shook off the sleepiness and raised my open palms toward Hank. "We're bros, Hank. Help me out here. It's too early. Can't you and Gracie give me a little more time?"

Hank reacted by leaping off my bed, sprinting into the hallway, and then vanishing. Gracie fixed her fierce gaze on me, but I avoided her eyes.

The sound of Hank's paws tapping against the floor broke the silence as he charged back into my room, his leash clamped in his mouth.

I shook my head in frustration, tossed aside my covers, and walked into the bathroom. They followed closely behind me. "At the very least, let me take a quick shower before we go for a walk."

I didn't let either of them protest with a bark, howl, or whine and stepped into the shower. Turning on the hot water, my wolves settled onto the cool porcelain tile of the bathroom, their eyes on me, waiting. My thoughts drifted back to one year ago when I discovered the abandoned wolf puppies on my way home from the local store. *They huddled together on the roadside, trembling and shaking, too young to be without their mother. Their bodies were mere skin and bones, and they had that look in their eyes that they were ready to give up. I tucked them into my jacket and rushed home, fully aware that my grandma would not be pleased with my impulsive decision, but I had to save them.*

My grandma's eyes widened in disbelief when she saw the little bundles of fur sticking out from my jacket as I walked in the door. "Ethan, did you bring wolves into my house?" She let out a deep sigh and was definitely annoyed, but as she noticed their desperate state, her disapproval began to fade. She quickly ushered me and the puppies into her clinic and examined them thoroughly. "I'm a physician, not a veterinarian," she said, "but these puppies are severely dehydrated and malnourished. I can give them fluids, and you need to buy puppy milk replacement from the feed store. Let Walter know they are wolf pups and about four weeks old. He will know what to give you."

Gracie's and Hank's urgent barks jolted me into the present and forced me to quickly finish my shower. Staring at myself in the double mirrors over the bathroom vanity, I saw bits of my grandma in me. We both had curly, caramel brown hair, although hers had strands of gray. The left corner of our smiles was slightly crooked, a trait that ran in the family. Our hazel eyes had more green than brown, and while she stood at 5'6" and weighed 125 pounds, I was taller at 5'10" and weighed 165 pounds.

She was a tough, 66-year-old woman with a strong personality who never remarried after my grandfather passed away. I never knew him. He died before I was born. Grandma, being the town's physician and surgeon, was accustomed to interacting with people and found comfort in those conversations. As for me—I was a loner and found socializing to be a challenge. I preferred the company of animals over people. Hank and Gracie were my best friends. All I truly needed was their companionship, along with my grandma's, of course.

When I was five, my parents left me at my grandma's house. That was fourteen years ago. We lived in Doford Peaks, a small mountain town in the state of Oakridge, with a population of around 1,200. With winter fully upon us, I dressed in utility pants, a long-sleeved T-shirt, and my winter boots to prepare for the cold. I also dressed Hank and Gracie in their waterproof winter coats and booties. Along with my down jacket, I grabbed a beanie and gloves. I stuffed my cell phone, inhaler, and compass into my pants pockets. With Gracie's and Hank's leashes in hand, I left my bedroom and dropped my jacket, beanie, and gloves on the entryway table.

Hank and Gracie followed me into our rustic kitchen, with exposed wooden beams and oak cabinets. Grandma particularly loved the large windows that allowed natural light to stream across the stone-tiled floor and the breathtaking views of the surrounding mountains. She was seated at the antique wooden table in the center of the kitchen, sipping a cup of coffee. Grabbing a granola bar and a bottle of water, I breathed in the rich aroma of French roast. "Morning, Grandma. You're up early."

"Ethan, good morning. A slight emergency brought me into the clinic." She sipped her coffee and continued, "LuAnn fell on the ice and sliced her hand open. She needed several stitches." Grinning, she said, "She asked about you."

"Please stop with the matchmaking."

"She's intelligent and attractive, much like you."

"That doesn't mean I have to date her."

"It doesn't mean you have to date her. But what's the harm in having a casual cup of coffee?"

"Being single works for me. Plus, I wouldn't know how to talk to her, and I wouldn't want to give her the wrong idea. Can we change the subject?"

She placed her coffee mug on the counter. "Fine. Are you going out for a walk with your wolf pack?"

I scratched Gracie and Hank behind their ears. "As much as I wanted to sleep in, they insisted I get up and take them for a walk."

Her gaze drifted to one of the large windows, where snowflakes were gently falling outside. Turning her attention back to me, she asked, "Do you have your inhaler?"

I patted my pocket. "Yes, Grandma."

"What about your cell phone?"

"I have that too."

"Since it's snowing, you should definitely take a jacket, and—"

My chin bobbed toward the door as I interrupted her. "I have a jacket, a beanie, and gloves."

"Hmm. What about water or a snack?"

I groaned and replied, "Grandma, I'm 19. I'm not a kid anymore. I can take care of myself."

A protective expression crossed her face as she placed her hand on her hip. "Ethan, no matter how old you get, in my eyes, you'll always be my precious grandson."

A sigh escaped my lips, and I shrugged my shoulders. "Do you want to just come with me?"

Her hazel eyes brightened with a smile as she waved a finger at me. "That's a great idea," she said. "I'll get my coat."

Grandma came back wearing a down jacket. She was bundled up in winter clothing. A scarf was wrapped around her neck, and gloves covered her hands while she tucked her hair beneath the hood of her jacket. She grabbed a bottle of water from the cupboard and tucked it into her jacket pocket. Then she reached for Gracie's leash. "Gracie can come with me."

"Gracie is definitely easier to control than Hank. He tends to pull a lot, especially when he catches a scent." I handed her Gracie's leash.

"That's true!" she said with a smile. "I'm ready. It's beautiful right now. The sun is breaking through the clouds, the snow is falling, and the air smells of pine cones. What more could we ask for?"

"You sound like a greeting card, Grandma."

A chuckle escaped her lips. "I do, don't I?" She opened the solid wood door and replied, "After you."

Wood siding wrapped around my grandma's single-story home. The deep green roof blended into the surrounding trees, and the many windows let in tons of light, which my grandma loved. I led Hank through the doorway and onto the wraparound deck. We made our way down the stairs and onto the cement driveway. Continuing down the sloped driveway, we passed Grandma's clinic, a smaller replica of the main house. Glen's truck had cleared the road of snow. At 70, he was still going strong as the owner of a snowplow truck company. His silver hair was often dusted with snow, mirroring the bushy eyebrows that framed his kind, gray-blue eyes. Every time I saw him, he was wearing a flannel shirt, a heavy jacket, jeans, and boots. Maybe they were his favorites or maybe it was his uniform, but at least he was consistent.

We walked along the towering pine trees, now filled with snow, lining both sides of the road. The crisp, cool air stung my cheeks, so I pulled my beanie down as far as possible and still be able to see. Hank and Gracie strolled alongside us, their noses in the air, sniffing at whatever scents they could find.

Grandma asked, "Would you like to talk about the letter your parents sent?"

"I don't," I abruptly replied.

"I think we ought to talk about it," she insisted.

I looked at her, hoping my expression conveyed my hurt, frustration, and exhaustion. "Grandma, I love you. I know my dad is your son, and

I don't mean any disrespect, but they handed me off to you fourteen years ago. Mom and Dad haven't visited me for any occasion—birthdays, Thanksgiving, or Christmas. They ghosted me! I couldn't care less about their stupid letters."

"I understand where you're coming from," she sympathized. "Although I don't support the choice they made, I know it was very tough for them to leave you in my care, and I can only imagine how confusing this all is for you. I don't know what your letter said, but in my letter, they reiterated their continued search for a cure for asthma. Their letter made it very clear that they're doing everything possible to help you live a healthier, happier life. I hope you know how much both your parents love you."

"Researching for fourteen years, Grandma?" I exclaimed, my voice filled with exasperation. "I'm sure even you don't even believe that."

"I know they love you."

"If they truly loved me, they would have been present in my life instead of concentrating on scientific research. My parents didn't want a flawed son."

Her hand touched mine as she paused. "Ethan, you can't possibly believe that."

"Regardless of what I believe, the fact remains that I have asthma, and I manage it. You stood beside me, not my parents. They've been absent most of my life. Even if they returned now, I probably wouldn't want to see them. I'm sorry, Grandma." I softened my tone. "My anger is directed at them, not you, and I'm just not ready to forgive them."

She hugged me tight and reassured me. "Ethan, I will always be here for you."

In her arms, emotions surged within me, and tears threatened to fall. Hank and Gracie surrounded me, nuzzling their furry heads against my body in an attempt to comfort me. As I pulled away, I admitted, "Talking about them doesn't help. It only makes matters worse."

"I understand how you feel. Everything is going to be okay, I promise. Let's continue our morning walk with Hank and Gracie and enjoy the day together."

Relieved, I nodded, and we continued down the road. Hank and Gracie glanced back at me occasionally to ensure I was okay. As we walked, the various smells around us began to capture their attention more than my presence. They trotted happily alongside me, their snouts pressed to the pavement, wagging their tails as they sniffed every tree.

"It's chilly today," Grandma said and shivered and then glanced at me. "How are you feeling? Any shortness of breath?"

"So far, so good, but I agree it's super cold. Maybe we can cut our walk short."

"Good idea, and I agree."

Hank suddenly stopped, raised his nose, and howled. A few birds scattered from the branches above, startled by his abrupt call. Had he sensed something: an approaching storm or another animal nearby? Gracie's ears perked up as she lifted her head and let out a softer but equally determined howl. My wolves stood side by side, their eyes scanning the horizon, alert to something I couldn't see. Hank started tugging on his leash, and I pulled backward. "What is it, Hank?"

"I don't see anything," Grandma said, glancing around the area.

I peered between the trees, searching and feeling compelled to understand what Hank and Gracie were sensing. "They definitely smell something. Let's check."

"I am not sure if it is safe, Ethan."

"Grandma, we need to investigate. If it's an injured animal or more abandoned pups, we can call Marsha and have her send her wildlife team out here."

"Fair enough." Grandma nodded.

I released the slack on Hank's leash and commanded, "Find it!"

Hank and Gracie raced ahead, tugging Grandma and me along. Our breaths rose into the air like swirls of smoke. Frost covered the road, crunching beneath our boots as we followed my wolves. As we went down the road, the trees got thicker and thicker, reaching up to the pale sky, casting shadows, and blocking out the sun.

My wolves' noses skimmed along the damp earth, sniffing. Occasionally, they paused to circle a spot several times before continuing on their determined path with their noses once again on the ground. They sped up and tensed their bodies as they focused on the trail that led us up the hill to a cliff that looked like the entrance to a cave.

Despite the cold, beads of sweat formed on my forehead, and a tightness spread across my chest. The familiar constriction gripped my lungs the higher we climbed. I couldn't wait any longer. I needed my medicine. Fumbling in my pocket, I reached for my inhaler. I could feel Grandma's eyes fixed on me as I struggled to breathe.

Grandma's voice was tense as she ordered, "Stop and use your inhaler. You're having trouble breathing."

"Hank is pulling me too hard. I can take a puff while I'm moving."

"Nonsense," Grandma said, taking Hank's leash from me and bringing both Hank and Gracie to a halt. The wolves howled in protest. "There, now they've stopped. Please, Ethan, use your inhaler right now, and I mean it."

I didn't argue and put my inhaler in my mouth, pressed the button, releasing the medication, and breathed deeply. After a few seconds of inhaling and exhaling, the pressure lessened, and I put my inhaler back in my pocket. Gradually, the tightness in my chest vanished.

"Better?"

I nodded.

"I can't risk your health for Hank and Gracie to chase down some scent. We need to turn back."

"No, Grandma! I'm fine. If there's an animal in trouble, we need to save it. I'll never forgive myself if we don't keep going."

Her lips formed a thin line, and her brow furrowed with disapproval. Grandma knew that Hank and Gracie were not just my pets. They knew me better than any human. They were part of our family. I felt a deep responsibility to protect all animals, and my grandma knew that.

Again, I begged, "Please, Grandma."

After several minutes of hesitation, she finally responded, "We'll proceed, but if you have another episode, we're finished." She handed Hank's leash back to me.

I let out a sigh of relief. "Thank you. I'll be okay. I promise."

She huffed and waved me forward.

After hiking up the hill, we arrived at the cave, its dark entrance framed by jagged rocks. A thick fog floated within the darkness, reminding me of dry ice. I had my doubts about going inside. The cave floor could be unstable or wild animals could be hiding inside. And what if the air was thin and stale and triggered my asthma? But Hank and Gracie were insistent, pulling on their leashes to get closer.

Peering into the cave, Grandma asked, "Did you bring a flashlight?"

"No, I didn't," I replied, my eyes widening as a thought struck me. "I can use the app on my phone."

When I pulled my phone out of my pocket, Hank leapt forward, yanking his leash from my grip. Gracie followed suit, breaking free from Grandma's hand and racing after Hank. I switched on the flashlight app, flooding the cave with light. The beam flickered across dirt and jagged rocks. I pointed it upward, and Hank and Gracie running down a narrow passageway fell into view. The musty stench and distant sounds of water dripping grew stronger as we followed them.

"They must have found the source," Grandma said, matching my pace.

My heart raced as fear tightened in my throat at the thought of something harming my wolves. "I'm freaking out," I blurted, trying to keep my phone steady with trembling hands. I had no idea what this cave contained, whether it was safe, or what Hank and Gracie had stumbled upon. They never disobeyed me. Maybe Grandma was right about turning back.

"They'll be fine. They're strong creatures. Just try not to worry."

"I'm trying not to."

Hank barked sharply, his call signaling to me that he needed me. I rushed blindly into the cave, adrenaline coursing through me. The sound of Grandma's boots brushing against the cave floor echoed behind me as she ran.

The flashlight beam caught something ahead, but the darkness obscured my view. Upon closer inspection, I saw Hank and Gracie circling something on the ground. Slowing down, I hoped it wasn't an injured animal. As Grandma reached the spot ahead of me, she gasped. I stood still, unable to take another step. "Grandma, what's going on? What is it?"

As her gaze turned toward me, she said, "Not a what, but a who. It's a young woman, maybe 18 or 19 years old."

"What?" I rushed forward, closing the distance to the scene. I halted just behind Grandma, who was kneeling beside an unconscious girl, curled up in a fetal position, wearing a hospital gown. Hank and Gracie stood close by. Her long strawberry blonde hair was a matted, tangled mess hanging over her face. Her pale skin stood out in contrast to the bruises and deep red cuts all over her arms, legs, and especially her bare feet. Pus oozed out of them.

Grandma was in full-on doctor mode, checking the girl's pulse, listening to her breathing, and examining her numerous wounds. As she assessed the girl's condition, her eyes narrowed in concentration.

"Jesus," I whispered. "Is she alive?"

"Her pulse is weak, and her breathing is shallow, but she's alive," Grandma confirmed, her focus on the girl. "Her body temperature is low. It could be hypothermia. She's wearing a wristband, but it's not from the hospital in town." She turned to me. "Give me your jacket. She needs to warm up."

I removed my jacket and handed it to Grandma, who carefully wrapped it around the girl.

"We need to get her out of here and to my clinic immediately," Grandma urged. "We can't carry her, and I need my medical van. You'll need to keep a close watch on her while I go get the van. Be prepared that you may have to perform CPR if her heart stops."

My jaw dropped slowly as the weight of responsibility washed over me, sending a wave of anxiety coursing through my body. The thought of performing lifesaving measures on someone was terrifying. What if I screwed up? "I'm your bookkeeper. This is beyond my capabilities," I said, gesturing toward the girl. "I can't help her."

"You can handle this. Besides, we've trained many times on all emergency procedures."

The cave felt as if it were closing in around me. Memories of Grandma's first aid lessons flooded my mind, each one a jumbled mess of instructions and distant recollections. I shook my head firmly. "No, I can't do it. What if she wakes up and sees some guy standing over her? You know I'm not comfortable with people. She'll probably freak out. Just let me go get the van, and you stay here."

Grandma looked at me, as if weighing my suggestion, but her expression remained firm. "I understand your hesitation, but she needs medical treatment immediately. You'll have to run to the house, Ethan. I can't risk you having an asthma attack. It's better if I go."

The thought of being alone with an unconscious stranger filled me with anxiety. What if I made a mistake and ended up making things worse instead of better? What if her injuries worsened, and I wasn't able to save her? Every rational part of me screamed at me to let Grandma handle it. I had to be the one to get the van. "I've hiked trails many times—maybe not up a mountain, but I've covered long distances without an episode. Plus, I have my inhaler. Please let me get the van, Grandma."

She studied me for several minutes, probably envisioning various scenarios and their likely outcomes. After sighing, she relented. "All right. The keys to my van are in my office in the top drawer on the right side of my desk at the clinic, not my home office."

I nodded and turned to leave but quickly faced Grandma again. My gaze shifted to Hank and Gracie. Instead of coming with me, they remained by the girl's side. My brows furrowed in confusion. Why had they tracked her in the first place, and why were they so protective of her? Was it her injuries? The blood? The situation? It didn't make sense.

"Ethan, what's wrong?" Grandma asked, interrupting my thoughts.

I glanced at her before shifting my focus back to my wolves. "Hank and Gracie," I said. "It's odd how they're behaving. They don't even know this girl that they're trying so hard to protect."

"We can figure that out later. Right now, we need to get this girl to my clinic." She waved me away. "Go now and hurry back. Stay safe."

"I will." I cast one final glance at Hank and Gracie before hurrying out of the cave.

Chapter 2

The hill was not too steep, but the frost made it impossible to run down. I skidded down with my boots acting like skis, grabbing onto branches now and then to prevent myself from falling. I shivered without my jacket as the cold air seeped through my long-sleeved T-shirt and stung my skin, but I couldn't think about that. It didn't matter. Grandma depended on me to get to the van, and every second without warmth and treatment could worsen the girl's condition.

Once I reached the bottom of the hill, a gentle breeze rustled the tree branches, causing more snowflakes to fall onto the road. I broke into a light jog, careful not to overexert myself and trigger my asthma. Even though I was covered in snow, running generated enough heat to keep me warm and reduce the chill.

While focusing on the horizon, I breathed in and out slowly, just as Grandma had taught me when I was young. *Her soothing voice guided me through each breath as I sat with her on the porch. She would say, "Breathe in the good, breathe out the bad," encouraging me to visualize the air rushing in and out of my lungs, carrying away any tension.* Those exercises had helped prevent and calm my episodes. Running home, I let those words fill my head. When I saw our house, relief washed over me, and I ran up the wooden steps. I paused for a second to catch my breath and then ran inside to find Grandma's keys. In the mudroom, I quickly grabbed the clinic key from its hook and dashed toward Grandma's office in the clinic. The van keys were exactly where she said they would be.

I bolted outside toward the parked van, clicking the remote as I hopped into the driver's seat. Before starting the engine, I suddenly remembered something and jumped out of the van. I pulled open the side door, flipped on the heat switch for the gurney, and piled some blankets on top. I hoped the added warmth would help raise the girl's temperature. As I prepared to pull out of the driveway, I muttered, "Thank God for all-wheel drive."

A five-minute drive brought me back to the site, where I parked the van along the side of the road. After retrieving the rescue basket stretcher from the van, I laid it flat on the pavement. The basket seemed the most appropriate way to carry the girl down the hill. I pulled the basket up the side of the hill with me. The ground was uneven, which made it hard to keep my balance, and the snow kept getting stuck in the basket, which made the job even harder. Sweat drenched my body, and my chest throbbed as I finally reached the top of the hill. Fortunately, it wasn't a full-blown asthma attack. I didn't want Grandma to panic, so I took a moment to steady my breathing before heading into the cave.

Once inside, I rushed toward the girl, Grandma, Hank, and Gracie. Everything appeared unchanged, but I still asked, "How is she? Has she woken up yet?"

Grandma grimaced and shook her head. "She hasn't regained consciousness, but she does seem warmer since putting on your jacket."

"That's a good sign, right?"

"I won't know until I get her back to my clinic and examine her thoroughly." She glanced at the basket. "Good thinking. We can use it to transport her safely."

"I turned on the gurney's heater in the van and covered it with blankets, hoping it would generate enough warmth to raise her body temperature."

Grandma smiled. "And you thought you couldn't do anything to help her."

Shrugging, I replied, "That stuff is simple. CPR is on an entirely different level."

"Well, I'm proud of you. You did great. Let's get her in the basket and back to my clinic. I'm also going to call Sheriff Reid to ask him to check on missing persons."

I nodded, confident that someone must be looking for her, especially since she appeared to have been in a hospital. I shifted my attention to the basket, which had a sleeping bag-like compartment designed for slipping someone inside. You could secure them with straps, ensuring they stayed in place. I just hoped the girl wouldn't wake up during the process and think we were trying to kidnap her.

"You take her feet, and I'll lift her shoulders, and we'll slide her into the bag and secure her," Grandma suggested before pausing and rising to her feet.

"What is it?"

"She's in a fetal position." Grandma pursed her lips and tapped her chin. "I was planning to straighten her out, but since I don't know the extent of her injuries, I think we should leave her in that position until I can get a CT scan."

I glanced at the girl and then at the basket. It was designed to lie flat, not to accommodate someone curled up like a ball. Although she was thin and not very tall, I doubted she would fit in her current position. "I don't know, Grandma. She might not fit curled up like that. Plus, if we don't distribute the weight evenly before going down that steep hill, the basket might tip over."

"While you make a valid point, I'm not comfortable with repositioning her just yet. Let's proceed slowly down the hill, step by step."

I shrugged. Grandma knew the medical stuff, not me, but that the basket was going to be a problem; there was a good chance it would tip over. "We could slide the basket along the ground," I proposed. "It would be less likely to tip that way."

In response, she waved a finger at me and said, "Great idea! I think that will work. Now, let's set her in the basket."

We secured the girl and carefully carried her through the cave, navigating the uneven ground until we reached the entrance and exited it. Our descent down the hill was gradual, with me in the front and Grandma at the back of the basket, skillfully maneuvering it through the snow. Gracie and Hank trotted alongside, their eyes intently focused on the girl.

Again, it puzzled me how protective they were of her. Hank and Gracie had always reserved their loyalty and protection for Grandma and me, never for a complete stranger. I turned to my grandma and asked, "Don't you find it strange how Hank and Gracie are acting around this girl?"

"They're being quite protective of her. Perhaps they sense something we don't," Grandma suggested.

"Maybe," I said, eyeing my wolves. They had limited interactions with people, which made it difficult for me to interpret the behavior they were displaying. Perhaps they did sense something, as Grandma suggested.

Grandma seemed to read my thoughts when she said, "They still love you, Ethan. You're their world."

"I'm okay," I replied, dismissing her concern with a wave of my hand.

A chuckle escaped her lips. "Ethan, your expression says it all."

I let out a sigh. "Let's just get down the hill."

"Very well."

With our boots sloshing through the snow, it took us an agonizingly long time to descend the hill. The cold seeped through our clothing, making each step more difficult than the last. By the time we reached the van, our hands were numb and trembling. My jacket was draped over the girl's hospital gown as she lay motionless, her pale face looking even whiter against the dark fabric. I could only imagine how she felt.

After placing the basket on the pavement, I opened the van's doors. I knew every second mattered as we moved her to the heated gurney. Grandma connected her to the monitor and then began reading her vitals.

"Her temperature is 92 degrees, indicating mild hypothermia. Fortunately, her heart rate, blood pressure, and oxygen levels are normal, which eases my concern slightly. The warmth from the gurney and blankets should help combat the hypothermia. After we transport her to the clinic, I'll administer warm intravenous fluids to help raise her core body temperature. Millie should be at the clinic already. I'm texting her to prepare the triage room for the CT scan I want to take."

I shrugged, unsure of what my grandma needed, but I was grateful that Millie would know. Millie was twenty when my grandma hired her, and that was ten years ago. Millie carried herself with confidence and had a calm and caring nature that put Grandma's patients at ease, something I lacked. I shifted my focus back to the task at hand. "Hank and Gracie will have to ride with you in the back. There's not enough room up front."

"As long as they sit on the bench and stay out of the way," Grandma said, her tone firm.

I pointed my finger at the seat and commanded, "Hank, Gracie, sit and stay."

The two jumped obediently into the van and settled quietly on the seat. After closing the doors behind them, I hurried to the driver's seat. Turning the key, the engine roared to life, and I carefully maneuvered it onto the road. A tight knot formed in the pit of my stomach, and I couldn't shake the feeling that she might not make it. Glancing over my shoulder at Grandma, I said, "We'll be there in five minutes."

***

The clinic was situated between the towering pine trees and the main house. By the time I pulled into the parking lot, the trees had already cast shadows over the entire snow-covered lot. I parked two spots away from Millie's car, and just as I opened the driver's door, Millie ran out of the clinic and hurried toward the van. She wore scrubs, and her dark hair was pulled back into a loose ponytail as usual. She acknowledged me with a slight nod, but her intensely focused blue eyes remained fixed on the side door. I stepped around her and pulled the side door open.

Millie grabbed the end of the gurney and assisted Grandma and me in lowering it to the ground. "What've we got?" she inquired.

"I'm not sure what happened to her," Grandma replied. "So far, I know she's suffering from mild hypothermia and cuts on her arms, legs, and feet are infected." Grandma pointed to the girl's wristband. "Have you ever seen a hospital band like this before?"

Millie shook her head. "It doesn't look familiar. Are you certain it's from a hospital? It could be from a clinic like yours or an outpatient center."

"She's wearing a standard gown, so I'm assuming it's from a hospital, but no, I'm not certain. Let's bring her inside. Millie, I need to get her height and weight, and then start her IV, run some labs, and get a CT scan."

"I have everything prepared and waiting for you."

I looked down at the girl. The most noticeable change was that she wasn't curled up in a ball anymore. "Grandma, she's lying flat. Maybe the heat helped."

Grandma patted my shoulder as she walked by. "It definitely helped. Good call, Ethan."

"Hank, Gracie, come," I called, following Grandma and Millie into the clinic as my wolves trotted alongside me.

While I held the clinic door open, Millie and Grandma pushed the gurney into the waiting room. The curved receptionist desk was empty, as Johnny, Grandma's medical receptionist, had not yet arrived. Johnny, who was only two years older than me, worked for my grandma for the past four years. Johnny always wore his dark brown hair neatly styled to one side and rectangular glasses. He never mastered getting contacts into his eyes. He always greeted my grandma's patients with a kind smile, something my grandma loved about him.

Through the hallway, we approached the double doors. Beyond them, the hallway branched into three distinct sections: the exam rooms on the left, the triage room on the right, and straight ahead, a fully equipped emergency operating room. They headed straight into the triage room. I never liked how the fluorescent lights cast a harsh sheen onto shelves stocked full of medical supplies in the triage room. It made everything feel so cold and impersonal.

It always amazed me how my grandma and Millie could communicate solely through nods. Together, they carefully transferred the girl onto the exam table equipped with a scale. "She weighs 112," Millie called out, then retrieved a measuring tape from the drawer and ran it down the girl's entire body. "5'4"," she noted. Millie activated the CT scanner, which whirred to life, while Grandma inserted an IV into the girl's arm. A faint but noticeable breath escaped the girl's lips as she lay motionless.

Leaving them to their work, I wheeled the gurney back to the van. Hank and Gracie trotted closely behind me. Their decision to accompany me rather than remain with the girl brought a smile to my face. After disinfecting the gurney, I locked it away in the van, wrestling with the guilt of feeling pleased that my wolves had abandoned her to come with me. Could I have been any more immature? My grandma was right. Why was I jealous of a stranger? The fact that they wanted to protect her didn't mean they loved me any less. That stupid thought clung to me as I took a deep breath. Even though it was absurd to feel threatened by their shift in loyalty, my jealousy persisted. Clearly, insecurity was something I needed to work on.

Organizing and stocking the van, I ensured Grandma had everything she needed for the next trip before returning to the clinic to check on the girl's progress. I entered the triage room about 15 minutes later. Millie and my grandma were standing on either side of the exam table. A bag of fluid hung above the table with a slow drip into an IV and then disappeared into her vein. Her complexion seemed less pale, and for the first time, I noticed she had freckles scattered across her nose and cheeks. While she seemed more relaxed, she still hadn't regained consciousness. She now wore a clinic gown and booties, so either Grandma or Millie had changed her. All the cuts on her arms and legs had been cleaned, and some even seemed to be improving, as if they were already healing.

"Grandma, did you notice that some of her cuts looked, um, I don't know, that they healed."

Grandma nodded in agreement. "Millie and I both noticed her progress. It might be due to the intravenous antibiotics we're administering and the wound flushing. She's young; her healing could be influenced by that or her genetics. Some individuals simply heal more quickly than others."

"Hmm. How's she doing otherwise?"

"The MRI showed no abnormalities," Grandma replied, sounding relieved. "Her oxygen levels are fantastic, her temperature continues to rise, and her organs are functioning normally. However, her blood showed abnormalities. I'm sending samples to the lab for cultures and specialized tests for proteins and enzymes to determine the cause. She might have a genetic condition that runs in her family or she might have been exposed to some toxins that changed the makeup of her blood. We might also be dealing with an autoimmune disease that is affecting her blood cells. It's hard to say what's going on right now until I get all of her lab results back."

"That's a lot," I said, trying to process everything my grandma had just told me. I was about to make a snide remark about how the girl would surely cringe when she woke up and saw the embarrassing booties on her feet, but a five-inch-long cut on the side of her right calf completely diverted my attention. The jagged line of stitches on her skin looked angry and painful. I pointed to the wound, asking, "What happened there, Grandma?"

"It seems something was removed from her leg. The dermal layer was also damaged, so I had to perform both internal and external stitches."

"What? They cut something out of her? Like a tumor or something?"

Grandma shook her head, her expression troubled. "I don't know," she replied, glancing at the girl with concern. "This poor thing has endured so much."

Johnny poked his head into the triage room. "Morning, everyone." He glanced at the girl on the examination table and asked, "Dr. Porter, you're fully booked after 11:00 a.m. Should I reschedule anyone?"

Grandma looked at her wristwatch. "I think we're fine, Johnny. Thanks for checking. Could you please call Sheriff Reid and let him know that we have a Jane Doe at the clinic and ask him to stop by?"

"Of course."

The door closed behind him as he retreated. My grandma finished typing her notes on her laptop and turned to Millie. "I've added the IV dose of cefazolin to her chart. You can administer her first dose while I check with Johnny about my schedule for today."

While my grandma confirmed her appointments, Millie double-checked the dose on the computer before administering it. I stood against the wall, staring at the girl lying motionless and wondering what her story might be. As I stared at her, her features drew me in. Even with everything that had happened to her, she was beautiful—thick, long eyelashes, freckled nose and cheeks, and soft pink lips. Her tangled mess of strawberry-blonde hair lay against the pillow. A warm feeling stirred inside me, and my heart fluttered. My curiosity grew as I wondered what lay behind her closed eyes.

I never had a girlfriend. My fate had been sealed since kindergarten, with my asthma scaring the other kids. As I got older, I became both a target for bullying and a source of amusement for my classmates. I was nicknamed "Asthma Boy," a label that certainly didn't help me get girlfriends. *In third grade, during a really bad asthma attack on the playground, I had to use my inhaler in front of everyone. I shoved it into my mouth as the kids around me chanted, "Asthma Boy, Asthma Boy." As they mocked me, my face burned with embarrassment. I wished I could have vanished or run away from them, but I couldn't move or breathe.* Though, as a teenager, the nickname "Asthma Boy" led to some pity-driven sex, but I never had a girl who genuinely cared about me. Eventually, I withdrew from everyone and blamed my parents for all the problems in my life. My parents didn't cause my asthma, but they also weren't there for me when I needed their support the most, so in my mind, that was just as awful.

A soft moan interrupted my thoughts, and I glanced at the girl. She stirred, and her eyelashes fluttered before slowly opening. Her turquoise eyes were full of confusion as they darted across the room. Her breath quickened, and she tried to sit up, her hands reaching for the IV line.

Millie hurried to her side, speaking softly to reassure her. "It's okay. You're safe."

A wave of asthma hit me, and my breath caught in my throat. Hank whimpered, and Gracie stood close to me. I grabbed my inhaler and quickly pressed the trigger, releasing a burst of medication that quickly eased the tightness in my chest.

The girl's eyes locked onto mine, narrowing in intensity. A flash of uncertainty crossed her face, quickly replaced by a grimace that resembled anger, even though I had nothing to do with what had happened to her. Hank whined again, this time louder, drawing her gaze. She shifted her attention from Hank to Gracie, her eyes widening in shock. Her lips parted slightly, as if she couldn't grasp what she was seeing. She whispered, "Wolves."

I nodded but didn't speak, as my lungs were still slightly constricted.

Although the girl seemed to understand the current situation she was in, Millie kept her hand on the girl's arm to prevent her from removing the IV. "You're in Dr. Porter's clinic. You're safe," Millie reassured her. "The IV is providing vital fluids and antibiotics for your infected wounds." She pointed to the girl's wristband. "It seems you were hospitalized previously, but the wristband does not indicate the name of the hospital or your name. I'm Nurse Millie. Can you tell me your name?"

My grandma entered at that moment and immediately noticed the change in circumstances. In her calm and soothing doctor's voice, she said, "I'm Dr. Porter. This is my clinic. I see you've met my nurse, Millie." My grandma gestured toward me. "And that's my grandson, Ethan. Beside him are his pet wolves, Hank and Gracie."

I waved at her, only to feel a rush of embarrassment. The girl's puzzled expression only grew more pronounced, and I quickly lowered my hand, wishing I could vanish like when I was back in grade school.

When my grandma approached the exam table, Millie moved aside. Grandma took the girl's hand in hers and gently asked, "Can you tell me your name?"

"Mia," she replied quietly. "Mia Rowe."

Finally, a name. Now I could stop calling her "the girl."

"Do you remember the hospital where you were before?" Grandma asked. "The wristband didn't provide much information."

"I—I don't remember."

"Were you ill or maybe you had surgery while in a hospital?"

She stared at the gown my grandma or Millie had put on her like it was a foreign thing. "I don't remember being in a hospital."

Grandma's eyebrows furrowed, and I thought she shared my concern. How could she not remember where she'd been? But she did seem pretty disoriented, and her eyes wouldn't stop darting around the room, making her distress obvious.

"Can you recall anything?" Grandma asked. "Like your address or maybe any family members?"

Mia bit her lip, and a deep crease formed on her forehead. "My mind's completely blank. It's like there's nothing in there."

"You were hypothermic when we found you," Grandma explained. "That can cause confusion, but it's temporary. Your blood work showed some abnormalities, but I won't know more until the samples come back from the lab. I started you on intravenous antibiotics for the infection in your feet."

Mia glanced at her feet, taking in the booties that surrounded them. She shifted her gaze back to Grandma. "My blood is being sent to a lab?"

"Yes," Grandma confirmed. "We should have the results back in a few days."

I noticed Mia visibly swallow. She seemed anxious about her blood being tested, but I couldn't understand why. Despite my lack of people skills, I decided to make another attempt at communicating with her. After I patted Hank's and Gracie's heads, I said, "Hank and Gracie found you. They picked up your scent and led us to where you were."

Her gaze shifted to me, and she asked, "Where was I?" Her voice quivered.

"You were in a cave, at the top of Mount Laurel, and unconscious," I explained, trying to sound reassuring. Her eyes grew wide as she stared at me. "But as Millie and Grandma said, you're safe now," I added.

She just stared at me for a few seconds before turning her attention to my grandma. "What's going to happen to me now?" she asked.

"What a strange question," I thought, considering that we had just reassured her she was safe. It was as if she expected some form of punishment. Relief would have been a more normal response, wouldn't it?

"We will continue monitoring you and treating your infection," Grandma enlightened her. "But I want to transfer you to the hospital for at least a day or two while I wait for your lab results."

"No," Mia exclaimed. "I won't go to the hospital."

Millie and Grandma exchanged glances. I knew what they were thinking. If she doesn't remember anything, why doesn't she want to go to the hospital?

"Can you tell me why you don't want to go?" Grandma inquired.

The tension in the room rose. Hank's and Gracie's ears perked up, sensing something was wrong. I scratched their heads, calming them down.

Mia remained silent, but the tenseness in her body revealed the turmoil she was in, like she was afraid or agitated.

"You must have been through a horrible experience," Grandma concluded.

Again, Mia said nothing. Hank moved away from me and toward Mia. His golden eyes looked up at her as he nudged his head beneath her hand. Mia's posture relaxed as she stroked his soft fur.

Johnny opened the door slightly and said, "Sheriff Reid is here."

"Thank you, Johnny. I'll be there in a few minutes."

"I'll let him know," he replied before shutting the door.

Mia's eyes flicked toward the door and grew extremely wide. "Am I being arrested?"

"No, Mia," Grandma said in a compassionate voice, "you're not in trouble. The sheriff is just here to check on the situation."

Ever since she regained consciousness, Mia had seemed jittery and paranoid, as if she might flee at any moment. What was fueling her paranoia? Clearly, a memory tormented her, suggesting that she did recall something, and Sheriff Reid's arrival only exacerbated the situation.

"We need to resolve your hospitalization issue before I talk to Sheriff Reid," Grandma stated firmly. "Given your memory loss, I don't think you'll be able to provide me with the name of someone who can take you in and care for you."

"There's no one," she replied.

"Mia, you'll need to stay off your feet for at least two to three weeks. During this time, you'll need help with getting around, changing your dressings, and fixing your meals, to name a few things. Unfortunately, I don't see that I have any other choice but to send you to the hospital."

Mia's hands clenched, and her breath quickened. I didn't understand the cause of her panic, but whatever it was, it seemed serious. Maybe she'd had horrible experiences with hospitals, which would explain why she was adamant not to go to one. It was so obvious that she wanted nothing to do with any hospital and probably would refuse to go, and that's when an idea popped into my head. Before I thought it through, I just blurted it out. "She can stay with us, Grandma."

"Ethan!" Grandma gasped.

Everyone stared at me as though I had just sprouted two heads.

Turning all lawyer-like on me, Millie said, "There's a conflict of interest here, not to mention ethical codes and professional guidelines. That could put your grandmother in a difficult position, Ethan."

Despite my struggles with social interactions and my tendency to be a loner, my offhand suggestion came from a place of compassion. I hadn't thought about the legal stuff. I just wanted to provide Mia with some support, especially since hospitals freaked her out.

"Maybe I could rent a place," Mia said quietly. Her voice grew stronger as she added, "I'm 18, so I'm an adult. Dr. Porter, if you make house calls, that should resolve any legal issues, right?"

Millie lightly nudged my grandma's shoulder and said, "Glen and Sarah have that one-bedroom cabin they've been trying to rent out."

Grandma smiled and replied, "That could be a good option."

Mia got out her phone. "I'll text Glen and let him know he might have a potential tenant."

Huffing, I crossed my arms over my chest. "Does anyone else see what's wrong with this picture?"

"What?" Millie asked, shrugging.

I glanced at Mia and said, "Well, first of all, she has no identification. Second, no offense, but you didn't actually show up with any money. Last I checked, both identification and money are necessary to rent a place."

"Ethan," Grandma chided, "where are your manners? You should apologize."

"I'm not being rude. I'm just stating the facts, Grandma."

"He has a point," Mia admitted. "I don't have any identification, but I'm pretty sure I have a bank account with money in it." She frowned, adding, "But I can't remember what bank."

My grandma patted Mia's hand and offered her a reassuring smile. "Sheriff Reid has a way of handling these types of situations. I should go see him." With that, she nodded and left the room.

Mia gently scratched Hank's ears and softly said, "Thank you, Hank, for finding me." She then shifted her gaze to Gracie. "You too, Gracie."

Hank remained focused on her as he stood by the exam table. Through thick and thin, Hank had always been by my side. Jealousy spread through my chest as I observed his loyalty to Mia. Was it possible that he sensed her vulnerability and that's why he chose to protect her?

Mia's eyes met mine, and a faint smile graced her lips. "If it hadn't been for you, Ethan, and your grandmother, I probably would have..." She shuddered. "Thank you so much."

Her expression showed that she understood how close she had come to death. I had faced that reality myself a few times due to my asthma. I knew I should say something comforting, but I wasn't very good at that kind of thing. One thought crossed my mind, so I voiced it, "You're safe now, and that's all that matters."

A pink flush warmed Mia's cheeks, and her eyes softened as she said, "Ethan, that means a lot to me."

I smiled at her. That was when I noticed Millie grinning at me. "What?"

"Nothing," she said, raising her hands in a gesture of dismissal.

"That wasn't nothing."

As Millie shrugged and turned away from me, I stared at her for several minutes. Did she think I had flirted with Mia? I would never flirt with a patient in my grandma's clinic. Hank was the smitten one, not me. I didn't know much about her. She was beautiful, but for me, what mattered was her character, and that girl had her secrets.

A knock echoed at the door, and my grandma walked in alongside Sheriff Reid. At 60 years old, he stood six feet tall, resembling a quarterback with his broad shoulders. Deep wrinkles framed his steel gray eyes, a testament to countless winters spent living in Doford Peaks. His sheriff's hat was a permanent fixture of his appearance, as was his neatly trimmed salt-and-pepper beard that covered his square jaw.

"Mia, this is Sheriff Reid. Sheriff Reid, this is Mia," my grandma said, gesturing toward both of them.

Nodding, he said, "Hello, Mia. Dr. Porter updated me on your situation. I understand you've been through quite an ordeal. My team is currently conducting a search through the databases of the National Missing and Unidentified Persons System as well as the National Crime Information Center. Do you mind if I ask you some questions?"

Mia's face flickered again with anxiety, and she hesitated but replied, "Okay."

He held up the wristband that she had been wearing. "Dr. Porter informed me that you were wearing this wristband when she and Ethan found you," Sheriff Reid explained, his voice gentle. "This wristband could possibly be from a military hospital. Can you clarify if that's accurate?"

She gripped the edge of the blanket tightly, her gaze darting between Sheriff Reid and the wristband. "I don't remember."

"Even the smallest bit of information might help us piece things together. Do you recall any involvement in military operations?" He paused, giving her a moment to collect her thoughts.

Her voice trembled as she responded, "I wish I could remember, but I just can't."

Sheriff Reid's cell phone rang abruptly, and he stepped toward the back of the room to answer it. "What do you have for me, Vance?" He held the phone close to his ear, and for several minutes he just listened, and then asked, "What? No hits?" He glanced over at Mia. "I believe I have a fingerprint kit in the shop. I'll follow up with you shortly." After ending the call, he approached the exam table. He was calm, but his eyes were on fire, as if he knew something. "Is there anything you haven't told me, Mia?"

"No, not that I'm aware of," Mia replied, kind of standoffish.

"The name Mia Rowe does not appear in any database," he explained. "My team also searched social media. They found several individuals named Mia Rowe, but none were in the United States or matching your description. We might have better results with fingerprinting or DNA testing. I suggest we move forward with those."

Her shoulders tensed as a faint flush crept up her neck. "May I ask a question?"

"Of course."

"Umm," she cleared her throat. "Will other agencies know that you entered my name into these databases or if you run my fingerprints and DNA?"

Sheriff Reid narrowed his eyes and tilted his head. "That leads me to believe you remember something."

Gloom settled over her face, as if she was hiding something she wanted to protect. She replied, her voice low. "No, I don't remember anything. It's just that I have this feeling like I'm not safe."

There it was again, the paranoia. I fought the urge to blurt out, "*What happened to you? I know you remember. Just tell us!*" Maybe she feared the consequences or perhaps she thought we wouldn't believe her. I wondered if she was protecting someone or if she was simply too overwhelmed to confront the truth herself. Whatever the reason, her silence left us all in the dark.

Sheriff Reid appeared to share my concerns as he asked, "Can you elaborate on that feeling? Do you feel stalked or threatened?"

Tears filled her eyes, and she blinked them away. A single tear escaped, rolling down her cheek. Her hands clenched into fists as she took a shaky breath. "Every time I try to remember, there's this fog in my head that just gets thicker." Her voice sounded desperate. "It's like my mind refuses to let me remember."

"We need to establish your identity. I believe our most effective approach is to proceed with fingerprinting and a DNA test. To answer your question, we typically inform other law enforcement agencies when we conduct searches in national databases."

She shuddered, drawing her legs tightly to her chest and wrapping her arms around them.

"I assure you that we can provide protection for you," Sheriff Reid confirmed.

Then Millie spoke up, saying, "I texted Glen to let him know that Mia might be a possible tenant. He just texted back that he's open to it."

Sheriff Reid nodded in agreement. "Glen's place is well guarded with surveillance. I can station a deputy there to provide additional security."

She looked up at Sheriff Reid, her eyes seemed to fill with hope, and her body relaxed slightly. "Thank you. I guess we can move forward with the tests."

CHAPTER 3

Hank spent most of the night whining and pacing by my bedroom door, not understanding where Mia had gone. I couldn't get him to relax, and he kept me up most of the night. When morning finally came, I gave up on sleeping and got up. I had already taken him and Gracie for a walk, made enough breakfast for me and Grandma, and brewed a pot of coffee.

Sitting at the kitchen island, I sipped my coffee while waiting for my grandma to wake up. I had a question in mind: Could I go to see Mia? If Hank could see her, that would probably calm him down. Mia didn't have a cell phone, so I had no way of contacting her, and I couldn't just show up, but Hank needed to see her. My grandma could call Glen or Sarah, and they could ask Mia. I took another sip of coffee as I mentally rehearsed what I planned to say. *Grandma, Hank is freaking out! He's worried about Mia, and I thought seeing her would calm him down. The problem is, I can't call Mia. Could you call Glen or Sarah and ask them to ask her?*

As I practiced my speech, my grandma walked into the kitchen, dressed in a light blue blouse and gray slacks. She had her doctor's coat draped over her arm. After hanging her coat on the back of one of the chairs, she greeted me with, "Good morning. You're up early."

With a shrug, I nodded. "Morning. Hank was restless. I was up most of the night." I pointed to the stove. "Eggs and potatoes are warming on the stove."

Her gaze moved to Hank and Gracie lying at my feet. "Maybe he could use a walk."

"Been there, done that."

"How long have you been up?"

"Since 4:30, so about two hours."

"Oh, my goodness, Ethan." She bent down, gently stroking Hank's head. "Poor baby," she murmured before petting Gracie.

"Can I bring him to see Mia?" I blurted out, abandoning the speech I had planned.

A look of suspicion crossed her face as she stood up.

I needed to explain quickly. "Hank got close to her, and now she's not here, and he doesn't understand why. I think he senses that something terrible has happened to her. I want to show him that she's okay so he can shake off this restlessness. Would that be okay?"

While pondering my question, she poured herself a cup of coffee. After taking a sip, she responded, "We'll need to check with Mia. Glen's probably out on the road, so I'll text Sarah and ask her to check with Mia."

"That would be wonderful, Grandma," I replied, feeling a wave of relief. The last thing I wanted was another sleepless night caused by Hank's restlessness. "When can you text her?"

"Ethan, it's only 6:30 in the morning. Let's wait until 9:00 a.m."

I sighed. "Okay."

Bringing her breakfast to the kitchen island, my grandma sat down beside me. She took a forkful of eggs and potatoes and stuffed it into her mouth. "Mmm, that's delicious, Ethan."

My pride swelled as I replied, "Thank you. Breakfast is one of my specialties."

"It certainly is."

Changing the subject, I asked, "Has Sheriff Reid gotten back to you about her fingerprints or the DNA test?"

She shook her head. "He hasn't responded yet, but I think it's still too soon. These tests can sometimes take two to four weeks. However, we did run a rapid DNA analysis, and those results typically come back in less than two hours, so I'm not sure why we haven't heard back on the rapid test."

"Do you think she lied about her name?" I asked, still filled with doubts about Mia. "She seemed genuine, but you can never be certain, especially with someone you don't know."

"That's for Sheriff Reid to determine. My role is simply to ensure she heals and regains her strength." She looked directly at me. "She's alone here and has been through a lot. She might need a friend, Ethan."

A friend? As a loner, my people skills were almost nonexistent, and friendships didn't come easily to me. My childhood experiences taught me to distrust others because they were often cruel for no reason. The very idea of forming a friendship triggered my old insecurities and fears of rejection. I wasn't sure I was capable of being that friend, but something about Mia's vulnerability drew me in. Maybe she was different from others.

***

Thankfully, Mia agreed to let Hank, Gracie, and me stop by around 1:00 p.m. I rummaged through my closet, tossing shirts across my bed. I changed my shirt six times, trying to find the perfect look. Then I froze, a frown creasing my forehead. Wasn't I going to her place for Hank? Why did it matter what shirt I wore? It shouldn't have, though I felt the urge to impress her, even if I couldn't quite grasp why. Mia was a mystery, showing up out of the blue and with her own damage and secrets. Did trouble seem to find her? At the moment, I didn't care. There was something driving me toward her, making me curious to know more about her.

I pulled a long-sleeved blue Henley shirt over my head and slipped into jeans before lacing up my AF sneakers. Standing in the mirror, I studied my reflection. Was this the right look? I groaned and rolled my eyes. What the hell was wrong with me? I waved away my behavior and left my room to grab the leashes for Hank and Gracie.

The jingle of their harnesses sent them racing toward me, whining with excitement. They bounced around me, their paws bouncing against the floor, urging me to hurry. It took several attempts to get their harnesses on. After fumbling with the clasps multiple times, I finally managed to snap them together and then dressed them in their winter coats and booties before heading toward the front door.

Grandma called out, "Ethan, don't forget this," as she handed me my coat. "It's freezing out there. Do you have your inhaler?"

I slipped on my coat and sighed. "Yes, Grandma, I have my inhaler."

"Enjoy your visit with Mia. Please remind her about her recheck next Friday," she said, planting a kiss on my cheek.

"Sure, I'll remind her."

"Drive carefully, and text me when you arrive at Glen's."

"Grandma, he's only ten minutes away."

"It's snowing. Text me." The expression on her face indicated that it was not open for debate.

"Okay. Fine."

A light snowfall greeted me as I stepped outside. Before I settled Hank and Gracie into the back seat of my Jeep, they caught a few snowflakes on their tongues. Hopping into the driver's seat, I started the engine and engaged the 4WD. Glen's property was located halfway down the hill from my grandma's house, and you had to navigate a winding road to reach the main house and Mia's cabin rental.

During the drive, Hank sat alert, gazing out the window as if he understood where I was going. Gracie, on the other hand, was lying down with her head resting on the console. "Yes, Hank, we're off to see Mia, so let's keep the restlessness to a minimum tonight, okay? I need to get some sleep," I said, looking at him from the rearview mirror. He responded with a low woof.

A white mist covered the mountains, hiding their tops in the low-hanging clouds. I turned up the heater in the Jeep to keep the cold air from getting in. As I drove, the steady hum of the engine, the swish of the windshield wipers, Hank's panting, and Gracie's soft woofs surrounded me. When I turned onto the road that led to Glen's property, Hank jumped up.

As I drove slowly up the winding road, the tire tracks of my Jeep zigzagged behind me. There were tall pine trees on either side of the road, and their branches were drooping because of the snow. The traction on my Jeep stayed strong. After passing the main house, I drove for about 20 feet until I reached the cabin. I noticed a sheriff's SUV parked to the left of the cabin. Someone looked through the blinds in the front window as I parked. Before getting out of my Jeep, I quickly sent a text to my Grandma. Sarah, Glen's wife, opened the front door and stepped out onto the porch, waving me in. She looked like a librarian with her silver shoulder-length hair and her bright red glasses with thin rims.

"Hey, Mrs. Hodges. I'm here to see Mia," I said, opening the back seat to let Hank and Gracie out.

"Hello, Ethan. We've been expecting you." She gently patted Hank and Gracie on their heads, then again waved me inside. "Come in and get out of the cold."

Hank and Gracie trotted in just ahead of me as I entered the small cabin. The entryway radiated a warm, toasty vibe, much better than the chilly weather outside. I removed my coat and Hank's and Gracie's, too, along with their booties.

"Let me take those for you," Sarah said, reaching for my coat and hanging it on one of the hooks along the wall and laying my wolves' items on the bench. "Mia is in the living room." She pointed down the hallway. "It's just down that way."

As I walked down the hallway, I took in the wooden walls adorned with quilts and vintage photographs, giving the cabin a relaxed, lived-in feel. When I turned the corner, I entered the living room. An orange blaze flickered in a large stone fireplace. Anxiety rose inside me that the fire might trigger my asthma, and I paused for a moment, taking in a deep breath, testing it out. Fortunately, the burning smell didn't affect me.

Mia was sitting on a large sofa that occupied the back wall opposite the fireplace, wearing black leggings, a tan sweater, and furry black slippers. She had her feet resting on top of an ottoman. There was no more tangled, matted mess of hair. It had a beautiful soft sheen to it, and she wore her hair in loose waves down her back. Her face with all her freckles had a healthy, natural glow to it, and without any makeup. My heartbeat quickened as I stared. She looked beautiful.

As she glanced my way, a smile spread across her face. "Hello, Ethan."

Hank let out a high-pitched whine and dashed toward her, followed closely by Gracie. Mia leaned down to kiss each of their heads, wrapping her arms around them affectionately. My wolves squealed even louder when she greeted them with, "Hi, pups."

"Hi, Mia," I finally said as I settled onto the end of the sofa. "How are you feeling?"

Before she could answer, Sarah entered the room, accompanied by a deputy from Sheriff Reid's office. He stood with an imposing presence and was a tall man in his early forties, with observant, sharp emerald-colored eyes and a serious expression plastered on his face. Sarah gestured toward me and introduced, "Deputy Olson, this is Ethan, Dr. Porter's grandson."

He narrowed his eyes, studying me intently. Was he really screening me like I was a threat? Our town was small, and it wasn't uncommon to encounter unfamiliar faces. But seriously, was this guy for real?

Within a minute or two, he politely nodded and left, leaving me, Mia, and Sarah alone.

"Ethan, would you like some coffee?" Sarah asked.

"Yes, that would be great. Thank you."

"Cream and sugar?"

"Yes, please."

"Of course, I'll be back with your coffee."

Hank and Gracie lay down on the rug by our feet, cuddled up, and looked at us with their heads resting on their paws.

"To answer your question," Mia said, "I feel tired, and my feet hurt."

"I'm sure it will just take some time. By the way, my grandma asked me to remind you about your recheck next Friday."

She nodded. "I remember. Sarah said she would take me. The good news is that I finally got to take a shower, wash my hair, and ditch that hospital gown."

"No one can rock a hospital gown," I said, slicing my hand through the air for emphasis. "They're humiliating with the back open and your ass hanging out."

She giggled. "That's true."

A rich, dark, smoky scent filled the air as Sarah returned, carrying a mug. She set it down on a coaster on the coffee table. "Here you go. Just let me know if you need anything."

"Thanks, Mrs. Hodges," I said, taking a sip of my coffee.

"Of course." She leaned in closer and whispered, "I'll make sure Deputy Olson doesn't bother you two."

I couldn't help but smile. He was a bit of a downer.

After Sarah left the room, Mia and I were alone. A brief moment of awkward silence hung between us before I decided to break the ice. "Do you remember anything yet?"

She shook her head but remained silent. Discussing her past was something she truly seemed to dislike, so I shifted the conversation. "What do you think of the cabin?"

Her face brightened with a big smile as she looked around the living room and raised her hands in excitement. "I love it! I'm so grateful, especially to Glen and Sarah for letting me postpone my rent."

"They're good people. My grandma's known them forever, and I've known them since I was a kid."

Her brows furrowed slightly as she tucked a loose strand of hair behind her ear. It seemed like she was searching for the right words, her gaze flickering between the floor and my eyes. "May I ask why you live with your grandma?" she finally asked.

I stiffened and quickly tried to mask my nervousness. Should I share the long, drawn-out story of my life, give her the Cliff Notes, or simply refuse to answer? A familiar knot tightened my stomach, and I took a deep breath. Talking about my parents was never easy for me. I preferred to keep all that drama buried. For that reason, I settled on the Cliff Notes. "Well." I forced a smile. "My parents left when I was five, and my grandma took me in. They've never really been in the picture since."

"I'm so sorry," she said, with compassion. "I can't imagine how hard that must have been." She looked down at the floor and softly added, "At least you have parents. As someone who has been homeless, I never knew where I came from."

My head snapped toward her. Her cheeks were flushed, and her eyes darted nervously, refusing to meet mine. Had she suddenly remembered something from her past? Or was it merely a slip-up? While I couldn't be certain, her expression clearly suggested guilt. Yet Hank seemed completely captivated by her, and that wolf almost never misjudged people. Despite me suspecting she was hiding something, I chose to trust Hank's judgment. "Did you just remember something?"

She burst into nervous laughter. "I must have." She scrunched her face as if she had swallowed something disgusting. "When you mentioned your parents were out of the picture, an image flashed in my head: me, a seven-year-old me living in a tent on the streets. I was filthy, hungry, and alone, but that's all that came to me." She shuddered and crossed her arms tightly over her chest, shielding herself, possibly, from that memory.

Was there more, and she simply chose not to share the rest? As I studied her closely, I tried to tell which was the case. Her body language suggested she was troubled, yet her guarded expression looked like she was hiding something. But in that moment, I decided to give her the benefit of the doubt, even though I wasn't certain what to believe or if I should trust her. Not wanting to seem insensitive, I gently asked, "You really don't remember anything about your parents? Did they abandon you, or did you run away from home, and that's how you became homeless?"

She stared at me with horror etched across her face. Tears flooded her eyes, cascading down her cheeks. As she brushed them away, she cradled her knees into her chest and choked out, "I can't remember, okay!"

Hank leaped to his feet, resting his paws on the sofa while nudging Mia's arm with his head. Sarah and Deputy Olson rushed in. Mia's shoulders shook as she hid her face in her hands.

Sarah wrapped her arm around Mia, her gaze fixed on me. "What happened?"

"She remembered something," I replied, but a wave of guilt washed over me as I realized I had pushed her too hard.

"What did you remember?" Deputy Olson asked as he studied Mia's trembling body and my guilty expression.

"Being homeless. A memory suddenly overwhelmed me, catching me off guard. I'm sorry." She seemed to exhale all her emotions in a single breath.

"There's no need to apologize, dear," Sarah said as she placed her hand on Mia's shoulder. Here, let me make you a cup of cocoa. I feel that cocoa makes everything a little better."

Mia wiped away more tears and nodded. "Thank you, Sarah. I would appreciate that."

A knock at the door interrupted the conversation. Deputy Olson turned toward the sound, his hand instinctively moving toward his holster.

Sarah eyed her and then said, "Let's at least wait and see who it is."

Deputy Olson followed closely behind her as they both walked to the door.

When Mia and I were alone, I turned to her and said, "I shouldn't have pushed you. I'm sorry. I was just trying to help."

She sniffled, offering a half-smile. "It's okay. Remembering that was hard." She petted Hank's head and said, "Hank, I'm fine."

He relaxed and wagged his tail.

Several footsteps came from the hallway before Sheriff Reid entered the living room, along with Sarah and Deputy Olson. Standing in the center of the room, he fixed his gaze on Mia. "Mia, how are you feeling?"

"Somewhat better, thanks."

His tone grew serious as he said, "I have some news. The results of your fingerprint and DNA tests have come back."

I rose to my feet. "I'll give you some privacy."

Mia grasped my arm tightly. "Can you stay with me?"

I nodded and reclaimed my seat on the sofa beside her. Once she released my arm, she clasped her hands together. She resembled a tightly wound spring, ready to snap at any moment. Fear radiated off her, and she seemed to be struggling to hold herself together, so I pressed my hand over hers, and she clung to it.

"I'm ready to hear what you have to say."

Sheriff Reid met Mia's eyes, and his expression softened. "Well, it's not much, I'm afraid. Our database didn't match your fingerprints or DNA. Neither is on file. I know this isn't the answer you were hoping for. However, there are other avenues we can explore, such as genealogy databases, facial recognition, and a further review of social media and public records. We'll keep searching until we find answers."

Mia's calm expression suggested a need to erase her past, not recover it. To me, his news seemed like that was exactly what she had been hoping for. She quickly masked her relief with a sigh. "Thank you, Sheriff."

I came to the conclusion that Mia was either a ghost or her information simply hadn't been recorded in any system. Maybe she had adopted a new identity to shield herself from something or someone. Regardless of the reason, I had a feeling she remembered why and how she came to be in our mountain town, though I doubted she would ever state the truth.

Sheriff Reid tipped his hat to Mia and assured her, "Until we find a match, I will continue to ensure your safety."

"Thank you. I sincerely appreciate that."

Sheriff Reid nodded and exited the room, with Deputy Olson and Sarah following him.

I turned my attention to her and asked, "Are you okay?"

"I'm kind of relieved," she replied with a nervous giggle, her eyebrows rising as she looked at me. "If I were in the system, wouldn't that mean something more serious, like I'd committed a crime or something?"

With my lips pressed together, I tilted my head from side to side, considering her question. Maybe she really had no idea about who she was, and maybe I was wrong about her. "I see your point. I wish I could offer some sound advice, but I'm not very knowledgeable about identity searches."

Her hands fluttered briefly before settling in her lap. "I suppose I should have asked Sheriff Reid."

"You could ask Deputy Olson."

She shook her head and quickly gestured a *no*. "He isn't very friendly. While I appreciate his protection, he's really intimidating."

I smirked. "He definitely gives off some serious vibes." I nodded toward Hank and added, "But Hank wouldn't have taken to you if you were a felon. He has a good sense of character."

She smiled as she looked down at him resting at her feet. "I like him too."

Changing the subject, I asked, "So what's next? Are you planning to stay here in Doford Peaks?"

A bewildered expression settled on her forehead, and she bit her bottom lip. "I think so. I don't really have any place to go, or at least none that I can remember. But I need a job to pay rent. Without any identification, I'm not sure how that's going to happen."

I dismissed her concerns. "Don't worry about it. This is a small town where everyone knows each other. You might even be a local celebrity by now. Plus, many of the shops around here will pay their employees in cash."

"Well, that settles it then. Doford Peaks is where I'm going to put down my roots." She yawned and stretched her arms overhead, a clear sign of her fatigue.

She had been through a lot and mentioned feeling super tired, and I was keeping her from resting. That was my cue to leave. I rose to my feet and said, "I should go and let you rest."

She grasped my arm once more and pleaded, "Please stay."

As I gazed at her face and recognized the vulnerability in her eyes, it seemed as though she was afraid I might disappear the moment she let go of me. I wanted to stay, but I was also concerned about becoming too involved, especially given the fact that there were so many unanswered questions surrounding her past. I hesitated, not sure how to respond.

"I really want you to stay," she said, gently squeezing my arm.

Finally, I nodded and settled back into my seat. She released her grip on me and smiled brightly. "Maybe you can also stay for dinner?"

Dinner? I glanced at my smartwatch; it was just after 2:00 p.m. Our eyes locked, and I could see the plea in hers. She clearly didn't want to be alone. I recalled my grandma's advice before I left the house: She might need a friend. Sharing a meal could help ease her loneliness and might also provide me with a chance to learn more about her past. Besides, it seemed like the right thing to do. "Well, it is Tuesday, and I make a pretty mean taco."

Laughter sparkled in her eyes. "You cook?"

I brushed my knuckles across my shoulder. "I do. Are you up for Taco Tuesday?"

"Absolutely!"

Chapter 4

Taco Tuesday became a weekly thing, with me making the tacos, Sarah whipping up the refried beans and rice, and Mia offering scraps to Hank and Gracie, who eagerly accepted them. Mia and I talked like we had known each other for a long time. I loved how her eyes sparkled, how her laugh made me feel, and how warm she was. Spending Taco Tuesday with Mia was the best part of my week.

Mia's feet healed much too quickly, and my grandma attributed it to the antibiotics. Her lab results came back inconclusive, so my grandma still didn't have any answers. Sheriff Reid's luck wasn't much better. The additional searches didn't turn up anything, but Mia got a job at The Ice House, our local ice cream shop, thanks to his connections. The store needed her to have a phone, so I bought her a cell phone and helped her get it set up. Over the next few weeks, Mia and I spent nearly every day together. The more time we shared, the less awkward I felt around her. I hadn't quite figured out how just being around her made me breathe easier, but her calming nature seemed to be the reason my asthma attacks got better. And after two months of hanging out together, it wasn't just my asthma that she affected.

One Sunday night, watching a movie, everything changed. Scrolling through a list of movies, we'd landed on an old film called The Sixth Sense. I had never seen it, and Mia didn't remember any movies, so we decided to go with it. Sitting together on the couch, with Hank and Gracie fast asleep at our feet, a scene in the movie freaked Mia out. A girl in the movie suddenly appeared inside Cole's tent, and his breath turned cold. Mia gasped and grabbed my arm. I paused the movie and wrapped my arm around her. "It's okay," I said. "I'm here."

Her gaze locked onto mine as she gently brushed her lips against my own, kissing me softly. My heartbeat pounded inside my head, and I felt warm all over. At that perfect moment, the world around us vanished. Time seemed to freeze, and the only thing that truly mattered was that kiss, taking our relationship to a new level. Our bodies crashed into each other, and our hearts raced as our tongues touched. At that moment, I wondered if she felt the same strong feeling, the same electric spark that I did. We couldn't stop kissing, so I was pretty sure she felt the same way I did.

Hank's sharp bark pulled us apart. He and Gracie sat upright, tilting their heads and staring at us. I couldn't help but laugh, and Mia joined in. "Hank," I said, "this is what happens when you have a girlfriend."

Mia's gaze shifted from my wolves to me, a smile forming on her lips. "So, am I your girlfriend?"

I tucked a loose strand of her hair behind her ear and said, "I'd like you to be." I phrased it as a question, but it truly wasn't. I wanted her more than anything.

"I'd love to be your girlfriend." She cuddled up next to me and said, "I've never been in a relationship."

I jerked my head back and stared at her. "I can't believe that. Someone as beautiful, kind, and sweet as you should have guys falling all over themselves to be with you. Maybe this is just another part of your past that you can't remember."

Placing her hand over her heart, she nodded dramatically. "Oh my gosh, I'd definitely remember if I'd had a boyfriend—that feeling like you can't breathe until you see them again, and just thinking about seeing them makes your heart race."

"Is that how you feel about me?" I hoped she'd say yes.

"It absolutely is," she replied softly.

"I feel the same way," I whispered in her ear.

She kissed me, and pleasure rushed through me, throwing me off balance and spinning my head. Sitting there, wrapped in each other's arms, I wanted that feeling to last forever. When I finally pulled away, I confessed, "My life is so much better with you in it."

She giggled and nudged me. "I'm the lucky one. I know you could have your choice of girlfriends, but you chose me."

Her words triggered a memory of my high school prom, and one I'd rather forget. *Dressed in a dark blue tailored tuxedo, I arrived at my "supposed" girlfriend Jessica's house. On the passenger seat of my car sat a bracelet corsage made of orchids, which my grandma had helped me select. The delicate white orchids with purple trim my grandma said Jessica would love. Holding the corsage, I walked up to her parents' front porch, with my heart racing. When I knocked on the door, her father answered, looking puzzled. "Ethan, Jessica isn't here. She already left with friends."*

I stood there, speechless, as if he were speaking a language I couldn't understand. Finally, I managed to say, "I must have misunderstood her."

A look of sympathy replaced his confusion, and before he shut the door, he said, "Have a good evening."

Hunching my shoulders over my chest like a wounded animal, I hurried toward my car. High-pitched laughter and footsteps echoed behind me. I turned to see Jessica, Randy, Wally, and Freya standing there, all dressed in tuxedos and gowns. A smirk spread across Jessica's face as she taunted, "Did you really think I would go to prom with you?" She erupted into laughter. "I bet them," she gestured to the others, "that I could get you to sleep with me if I asked you to the prom." Her expression twisted in disgust as she shook her head, likely remembering when we had sex. "But I won the bet and collected $300, Asthma Boy."

My eyes brimmed with tears as I forced out the words, "So you're a whore?"

Randy's fist slammed into my face as he yelled, "Apologize, asshole!"

I collapsed onto the pavement, crushing the corsage beneath me, and curled into a fetal position, trying to protect myself as they kicked me over and over again. Each blow sent sharp pain radiating through my ribs. My lungs tightened, and I struggled to breathe. My breathing grew shallower and faster, triggering the all-too-familiar panic of an asthma attack with each desperate wheeze.

Jessica's father burst out of the house, shouting, "What the hell is going on? Jessica, get inside the house now! Boys, if you don't get the hell off my property and drive away, I'll go get my gun."

Randy grabbed Wally's arm, pulling him along, while Freya struggled to keep up in her high heels. They piled into Wally's car, scrambling over one another. Within seconds the tires screeched against the pavement as his car sped away.

Jessica stood there with her fists clenched, crying, the tears leaving dark streaks of mascara down her cheeks.

"Now, Jessica!" her father hollered at her. She hesitated for a moment, her eyes darting between him and me, before she broke into a run. The sound of her heels tapping against the porch steps lessened as she dashed inside the house and slammed the door behind her.

He knelt beside me and asked, "Do you have an inhaler, son?

Tears blurred my vision, and pain spread through my body. Unable to speak, I pointed to my car and handed him the keys. It took him several minutes to realize that my inhaler was in the glove compartment. He retrieved it, hurried back to me, and handed me my inhaler. My hands trembled as I clutched the inhaler and released two sprays. A moment later, my chest began to relax, and I was able to catch my breath. Without saying a word, he helped me up, led me to my car, and guided me into the driver's seat before walking away into his house. As I drove away, I felt humiliated and frustrated, and I could still hear the laughter and feel the betrayal.

"Ethan, are you okay?"

Mia's voice and her touch pulled me away from the past, and I shook off the painful memory. "I'm okay. I've been with a few girls, but I can't really call them friends, let alone girlfriends." I glanced at her. "Because of my asthma, I was the person everyone made fun of in school."

She stroked my cheek and shook her head. "You didn't deserve that, Ethan. Sometimes people can be so cruel." She looked into my eyes and declared, "I will always be here for you."

"You can count on me to be there for you, too." We gazed at each other for a moment longer, and then I asked, "Are you ready to continue the movie, or do you want to watch something else, like a comedy?"

"This one's fine. I'm ready."

After hitting the play button, I leaned back against the sofa and pulled Mia closer to me.

***

I left Mia's around midnight. On the drive home, the streets were quiet, but my mind wasn't. I couldn't stop thinking about Mia or our kiss. The romantic-looking sky with all the stars scattered through it and a full moon only added to my longing to be near her. She didn't look at me as a guy with asthma. She truly saw me for me. I had never experienced feelings like this with any girl. I'd only felt disappointment and hurt, but with Mia I was always on an emotional high, and I couldn't wait for tomorrow to see her again.

As our house came into view, my thoughts shifted to chatting with my grandma and hanging out with Hank and Gracie. From the garage, I entered the house through the side door and walked into the hallway. The familiar scent of lavender greeted me—Grandma's favorite. The house was always filled with that fragrance, thanks to the candles and air fresheners she kept around. Being out of the house for a while, the scent seemed overpowering and tickled my throat. I paused for a moment, but my breathing remained steady, and I continued down the hallway. All Grandma's favorite family photos lined the wall, and as I passed them, the wooden floors creaked beneath my shoes.

Grandma had a habit of falling asleep in front of the electric fireplace, so I checked the living room first. The plush sofa and chairs facing the marble fireplace were empty. The plush sofa and chairs looked so comfortable that I was tempted to sink into the cushions and fall asleep there myself, but a light coming from my grandma's office caught my attention. I headed in its direction, where I found her seated behind her desk, completely absorbed in whatever was on her laptop. I knocked softly on the open door. "Grandma, you're up late."

"Ethan, I didn't even hear you come in," she said, glancing up in surprise.

"I came through the garage. What are you working on at this hour?"

Her gaze shifted back to her laptop. "A colleague sent me a case he's struggling to solve." She gestured toward the chair across from her desk. "Have a seat. How was your night?"

A contented sigh escaped my lips as I sank into the chair.

"I see."

"There's something about Mia, Grandma. I know we're still getting to know each other, but I feel at ease around her, and my asthma has been under control lately."

Grandma's eyes softened, and a gentle smile came to her lips. "That's wonderful, Ethan. You should invite her to dinner. I would love to have the chance to talk to her, not just in a professional setting."

"That's an awesome idea! How about tomorrow?"

"I think I can manage it. What about 7:00 o'clock?" Grandma suggested. "Everyone will have gotten home from work, and I'll have plenty of time to make dinner."

"Perfect! I'll text Mia to let her know. Thanks, Grandma. I'm sure she'll love it."

"I'm looking forward to it."

I kissed her on the cheek. "Good night."

"Good night."

Hank and Gracie followed closely behind me as I rushed to my bedroom. Once I closed the door, I flopped down onto my bed, picked up my cell phone, and texted Mia. *Hey there! Are you up for dinner at my grandma's tomorrow night at 7?*

My heart raced when I noticed that she was typing.

Yes, I'd love to!

Great! I'll pick you up at 6:45.

Can't wait!

Night

Night

Changing into a T-shirt and boxers, I slumped onto my bed, with thoughts of Mia coming over for dinner filling my head. I wondered what my grandma was planning to make. Hopefully not anything fancy and formal. That was the last thing I wanted. Homemade lasagna, salad, and garlic bread popped into my head. That was more casual, and I had to remember to tell my grandma. If I wanted to sleep, I had to shut off my mind, but I just couldn't. For about an hour, I tossed and turned before I finally fell asleep.

As usual, Hank and Gracie woke me up bright and early, regardless of the fact that I'd only had a few hours of sleep. Groaning, I threw off the covers, took a quick shower, got dressed, and headed to the kitchen. I fed Hank, Gracie, and myself and brewed a pot of coffee for my grandma and me. With my coffee in hand, I left the house and made my way to my grandma's clinic and my office. I needed to reconcile bank statements, credit card charges, and patient payments. Several of Grandma's patients were on payment plans, and I needed to send out their invoices. I had a hard time focusing on the numbers in front of me because I kept thinking about Mia. By the time I finished my work, Johnny had already opened the clinic, Millie was busy setting up the exam rooms, and my grandma had just arrived.

"You certainly got an early start," Grandma remarked, peeking into my office. "Hank and Gracie?"

"Yep. They woke me up as usual." I then went directly to dinner and blurted out, "What are you planning to make for dinner tonight?"

"What would you like me to make?"

"Homemade lasagna, salad, and garlic bread."

"You've got it."

A sigh escaped me. "Thank you. I just want it to be casual—nothing over the top. I don't want her to think I'm desperate or trying too hard."

"Why on earth would she think that? Stop worrying. Everything will be fine."

"You're probably right." I groaned. "I don't understand why I keep obsessing over this."

"Because you have feelings for her."

I couldn't help but smile. "I really do."

"I can see how much she means to you. I have a full day at the clinic, but don't worry. I'll be home in plenty of time to start dinner."

Grandma was always there for me, unlike my so-called parents. She gave me peace of mind, and I loved her more than anything. A memory from middle school barged its way into my head: *Several kids had surrounded me on the playground, taunting me with that spiteful nickname, Asthma Boy. After I got home, I poured my heart out to Grandma, with tears streaming down my face. She held me and reminded me that I was strong. Grandma brought me into the kitchen and set everything out for us to bake cookies. The distraction was just what I needed to erase all the pain those kids caused. Having never baked before, I got most of the ingredients all over me and put way too much salt in the batter. We laughed, ate cookie dough, remixed without the extra salt, and made cookies together. I could always count on Grandma, no matter what.* The memory faded, and I wrapped my arms around her, saying, "I love you, Grandma."

Hugging me tightly, she echoed my words. "I love you, too, Ethan."

Johnny gently tapped on the door and announced, "Dr. Porter, your first appointment has arrived."

"Thank you, Johnny. I'll be right there." She turned back to me. "I'll see you later." She waved her finger at me and added, "And don't worry."

I laughed, feeling more at ease. "I won't. Thanks, Grandma. I'm heading home. See you later."

Walking home, the idea of browsing my bookcase crossed my mind. I hoped that reading would keep my mind occupied until dinner. I'd just walked through the front door when my cell phone chimed. It was a text from Mia.

Good morning! I'm excited about dinner tonight and can't wait to see you.

I was about to type, "I can't stop thinking about you," but hesitated. Should I really say that? Yes—wait—no. Wasn't there some unspoken rule in relationships that you shouldn't say how you feel too soon? My gaze was glued to my phone, but my fingers wouldn't move. Why was I acting weird about this? I groaned in frustration. *To hell with it; I'm saying it!* Despite the trembling of my fingers, I kept typing. *I can't wait to see you too, and I can't stop thinking about you.* Before sending my text, I added a kissing face emoji, a smiling face emoji, and several heart emojis for emphasis.

Oh my gosh, I feel the same way! I think about you every single second of every day!

As I read her reply, my heart fluttered, and I couldn't keep the huge smile from spreading on my face.

Sarah just dropped me off at work. I need to clock in, but I'll see you at 6:45 tonight!

I'll be there!

My pulse kept racing even after our texts had ended. Hank and Gracie trotted into the entryway, their tails wagging. I reached down to pet their heads and turned to Hank, asking, "Why am I so infatuated with this girl? You seem to be, too. What is it about her?"

Hank let out a low woof, but that didn't convey much to me. I had to figure this out myself. Was it her kindness, her genuine warmth, the way she made me feel seen, or the way she truly cared about every word I said? Maybe it was how her eyes sparkled whenever we were together, like I was the only person in the room. Actually, it was probably all of those things.

Hank and Gracie tagged along, following me into my bedroom. Standing in front of my

bookcase, I scanned the titles, musing over Pride and Prejudice, but then The Girl with the Dragon Tattoo caught my eye. I had been meaning to read it for a while. Ultimately, I decided on The Book Thief and pulled it off the shelf and brought it to bed with me, where Hank and Gracie settled in beside me.

My cell phone chimed again, breaking my concentration, and I glanced down at it. I didn't recognize the number, but maybe it was someone from The Ice House calling about Mia. At once I answered it.

The gentle tone of my mother's voice hit me as she said, "Ethan, hello. It's Mom and Dad!"

Shortly after, my father's gruff voice followed. "Hello, son."

My breath caught in my throat as I sat in stunned silence. They had purposely called me from some random number so I would answer. That was low, even for them. Anger slowly seeped into my veins, shaking my whole body. The urge to hurl my phone across the room tingled in my fingers, but I fought to keep my composure and forced myself to ask, "What do you want?"

"We just want to talk," my mother replied. "It's been so long. We miss you and want to know that you're okay."

I laughed out loud. "Give me a break! You abandoned me when I was five, leaving me with Grandma. You prioritized your careers over being present in my life. That absence created a gaping hole in my heart, and now that hole is filled with resentment."

"That's not true," my mother exclaimed. "We—"

My father interrupted, raising his voice. "We never abandoned you, not in any way, shape, or form. We're working night and day to find you a cure!"

"What difference does a cure make if you're not around?" I shot back. "I'm 19 years old and have spent most of my life without you. Grandma was the one who helped me cope. I think you both want this cure more than I do. What I needed was my parents."

"We want you to have a normal life. A cure will give you that," my father said, his voice thick with emotion. "We sacrificed all those holidays and birthdays, hoping to end your suffering."

In a quaking voice, my mother added, "We wanted to make a difference for you and others like you. It was a sacrifice we felt we had to make, but perhaps we lost sight of what truly mattered."

"There you have it," I spat. "Your real intentions are about fame. You want glory and a trophy for curing asthma."

My father yelled, "Enough! You—"

It was my turn to cut him off, and I shouted back, "You're damn right it's enough." I hung up and flung my phone away from me, my muscles tensing with rage. Simultaneously, my chest tightened, and raspy sounds escaped my mouth. My throat felt like it was swelling and cutting off air. Every attempt to breathe made my chest constrict.

My inhaler sat on my dresser on the other side of the room. I climbed off the bed and fell to the floor, lying helpless and desperate, paralyzed with fear. Terror surged through me, replacing the anger and resentment I had just felt. Would this be how I died—alone and gasping for air?

Hank and Gracie jumped off the bed and surrounded me. I could only gesture toward my inhaler, feeling completely overwhelmed. Hank followed the direction of my finger and dashed toward my dresser. He picked up the inhaler in his mouth and raced back to me, dropping it on the floor in front of me. I quickly grabbed it and sprayed the medication twice into my mouth. Nothing changed. I sprayed it again and then again. The struggle to breathe lessened, but the frustration and the pain my parents inflicted on me remained. Tears spilled down my cheeks, and I did nothing to stop them and just cried.

Hank and Gracie nudged me gently with their snouts, helping to lift me into a seated position on the floor. Leaning against my bed, I listened to Hank's soft whine as Gracie snuggled closer, her warm fur brushing against my skin. They hovered next to me, reminding me that I wasn't alone.

I pulled myself onto my bed and grabbed onto a pillow, hugging it tightly as if it were a person. Emotionally drained, I lay there limp, with Hank on my left and Gracie on my right. Once again, I let my parents get to me, pushing all my buttons. Would I ever learn? Hate filled me, and in that moment, I just wanted it all to stop and silence the haunting voices in my head. Fatigue finally took hold of my mind, dragging me into a deep, dreamless sleep.

The sound of my grandma calling my name forced me awake, and I found her sitting beside me on my bed. Looking into her eyes, that abandoned five-year-old boy resurfaced, and tears moistened my eyes—tears I couldn't control. I tossed the pillow aside and hugged her.

"Ethan, what happened?" she asked, her tone on edge. "Is it about Mia?"

I couldn't stop blubbering and simply shook my head to indicate "no."

She gently stroked my back, trying to comfort me. "I'm here. You're okay."

It took me several minutes to finally calm down enough to speak. I pulled away from her and shook my head again. "It wasn't Mia. It was Mom and Dad." I clenched my jaw as I shouted, "They tricked me into taking their call by using a different number. I was completely caught off guard when I heard their voices." I sniffled and wiped my nose. "We just argued, and I couldn't handle it, so I hung up on them. It made my asthma flare up, and I could barely breathe. If Hank hadn't brought me my inhaler, I might have died! Mom and Dad got to me, and I let them. I feel cheated, betrayed, and used. Of all days, it had to be today. My heart is shattered, and I feel broken and weak. I can't let Mia see me like this!"

With a firm yet tender tone, she said, "Ethan, look at me."

I looked into her warm hazel eyes, waiting for her to continue.

Taking my face in her hands, she said, "You're neither broken nor weak. I see pain in your eyes, but I also see determination. You have grown into a kind, remarkable, handsome young man. Some people might see you as stubborn, and there are times when you lack a filter," she chuckled. "But on the other hand, your heart is pure. Never forget who you are. Wash your face, change your clothes, and come help me with dinner."

CHAPTER 5

My grandma taught me that punctuality showed respect, and I made it a habit to always be on time. I valued my time as much as anyone else's. Waiting around for someone was the worst, so at 6:45 p.m. I arrived at Mia's. Before jumping out of my Jeep, I pulled my fleece jacket over my long-sleeved shirt, preparing for the chill. A light snowfall floated around me, and I hurried over to Mia's porch, brushing off snow as I knocked on her door.

Mia opened the door with a smile. She was wrapped in a cozy black-and-white checkered wool jacket. My gaze traveled over her outfit and quickly landed on her skinny jeans that hugged her body and the crop top with a bold white heart in the center, revealing just a hint of skin. Her high-top sneakers were super cool. Seeing her standing there, looking so hot, my heart raced. I shoved my hands into my pockets and said, "You look beautiful."

She giggled, her chin dipping slightly. "And you look handsome."

Taking her in my arms, I gently kissed her. Her arms came around my neck, drawing me even closer. The warmth of her embrace made me dizzy, but in a good kind of way. "Are you ready?" I asked, gesturing toward my Jeep.

"I am."

She slipped her arm underneath mine, and we walked toward my Jeep. Like a gentleman, I opened the passenger door for her and then jogged around to the driver's side. I glanced at her briefly, admiring how beautiful she was before starting the engine. The pain from earlier flickered inside me, trying to resurface. With a deep sigh, I pushed my parents from my mind. Tonight was about Mia.

"Are you okay?" she asked, her fingers gently resting on my arm. "You suddenly got tense."

"It was a tough day, but I'm alright now."

"Do you want to talk about it?"

"It's something with my parents, but I don't really want to get into it. Besides, just being with you, I already feel better."

She leaned closer and pressed a gentle kiss to my cheek. "I'll always be there for you."

I smiled, and after a few seconds of staring at her, I started the engine. Snowflakes floated in the beams of the headlights as I drove down the street. I had the heater blasting to keep out the bitter cold night. We shared a comfortable silence, stealing glances at each other, until I pulled into our driveway, clicked the remote control, and parked in the garage. We walked into the house, and smells of tomatoes, garlic, and cheese mingling with the faint scent of lavender greeted us. The hallway light cast a glow over the family photos. Not wanting to waste my breath discussing my parents, I quickly led Mia past the photos. Hank and Gracie dashed toward us, barking. Mia bent down to stroke their heads, and I followed suit.

Hank and Gracie trotted closely behind us, the delicious smells drawing us into the kitchen. My grandma stood behind the island, wearing her favorite floral apron over a black blouse and jeans. Her hair was pulled back into a bun, revealing gray strands at her temples. All the fixings for a salad were spread out on the cutting board in front of her. "Good timing, you two. The lasagna and garlic bread just came out of the oven," she said, tossing cherry tomatoes, cucumbers, and carrots into a large bowl of romaine and red leaf lettuce.

"Hey, Grandma," I said, popping a cherry tomato in my mouth.

"Dr. Porter, everything smells amazing. Is there anything I can do to help?" Mia asked.

"Please call me Evelyn. The only thing left to do is to take a seat and relax."

Despite her smile, Mia's expression conveyed a sense of, *I need to help you with something.*

With a playful wink, Grandma gestured toward a stack of plates and utensils on the counter. "If you're eager to lend a hand, you could help by setting the table."

"Of course!" At once Mia picked up the stack of plates and began moving around the table, setting places for the three of us.

I gazed at Mia, certain that a foolish grin was spreading across my face. If "drunk in love" really was a thing, I was undoubtedly a victim of it. Mia looked up, catching me staring, and her eyes brightened with a smile. My face flushed, and my heartbeat quickened, and in that moment, I realized how deeply I cared for her. This wasn't just infatuation. It came from my soul—genuine and true—and it made my heart race and my mind spin, and I never wanted that feeling to stop.

"Ethan, come grab the lasagna and garlic bread and set them on the table," Grandma said, carrying the salad bowl as she made her way to the dining table. She didn't forget Hank and Gracie. They each got a generous bowl filled with meat and plain lasagna noodles that they eagerly gobbled up.

"Sure," I replied, tearing my gaze away from Mia.

Grandma cut the lasagna into squares and placed a piece on each plate, along with two pieces of garlic bread and a bowl of salad. Before we started eating, she said grace.

Mia rolled her eyes in contentment, savoring every bite. "Evelyn, this lasagna is absolutely wonderful. The flavors are so delicious, and the cheese is just the right amount of gooey."

Grandma beamed with pride and winked at me. After all, it had been my idea for her to make the lasagna. She shifted her focus back to Mia.

"Thank you, Mia. How are things going at The Ice House? Are Ted and Ella treating you well?"

"They're both so kind, and it doesn't even feel like a job. I'm having so much fun there. Also, Sarah has been wonderful driving me to and from work. I think she's getting tired of hearing me tell her, 'Thank you,' but I hope to be driving myself soon. I'm saving money to buy my own car."

I was about to bite into my lasagna when I paused and then said, "You know you need a driver's license, right?" Without waiting for a response, I added, "And to get a driver's license, you'll need your birth certificate, social security number, and proof of residency."

Grandma raised her eyebrows at me. "Ethan, there's no need to be critical. Try being more supportive, please," she urged with a firm tone.

Mia waved her concern away. "It's okay. That's one of the things I like about Ethan. He's always direct and speaks his mind. You never have to wonder what he's thinking."

Laughing, my grandma replied, "That is certainly true."

In my defense, I said, "I'm not being rude. I'm simply stating the facts." To show I could be supportive, I added, "By the time you save enough money for a car, Sheriff Reid will likely have been able to verify your identity."

Mia nodded, her gaze flicking upward as if she were thinking. "That's true."

"I am sure he'll find information about you soon. He is an expert at what he does." Grandma affirmed.

"At least it's a goal I can strive for."

"Mia, that's very positive." Grandma looked at me. "Ethan, that's something you should pay attention to."

I showed my palms. "I'm positive." Her words took me by surprise. I may be blunt sometimes, but I've always seen the glass as half-full. The only thing I felt negative about was my parents. Is that what she meant? Maybe Grandma was just teasing, but it made me wonder if I should be more optimistic. I decided to press the matter. "Grandma, are you inadvertently trying to tell me something?"

"Not at all, dear. I'm simply saying that having a positive outlook can make even the most challenging situations feel more manageable and less overwhelming."

"Geez, Grandma. Can we keep the conversation light?"

"Very well, Ethan." She winked at me and turned to Mia. "Mia, I bet you're curious to hear more about Ethan."

"Absolutely! Do you have any stories to share?"

"No, no, let's not go there," I said, waving my hand dismissively.

Grandma smiled at me. "I'll tell you just one."

I let out an exasperated groan and rolled my eyes.

"Ethan is an excellent cook now, but he wasn't always. When he was a young boy, he made his first batch of cookies using salt instead of sugar." Grandma cringed as if she were tasting them all over again. "I ate one and then drank a whole bottle of water afterward."

A smirk spread across my face. "I remember that. The look on your face was totally priceless."

Mia's expression grew somber, and she looked down. "I wish I had something interesting to share about myself."

I reached across the table and gently squeezed her hand. "Hey, that's the best part about starting fresh, right? We get to create new memories." I smiled and added, "And I'm sure they'll be even better than my cookie disaster."

Mia laughed softly. As I glanced at my grandma, I thought, "See, I'm supportive."

A warm smile curved Grandma's lips, but the chime of her phone interrupted the moment. When she glanced at the screen, concern flashed across her face. "I apologize. I have to take this." She quickly rose from her seat and hurried out of the kitchen.

Mia's cell phone also vibrated, drawing her attention. "I just got a text from work. Someone called in sick, and they want me to cover the evening shift tomorrow. Sarah can't drive at night. Can you please take me and pick me up?"

"Only if I get free ice cream."

"Ethan!"

"I'm kidding. Yes, of course."

"Thank you. I'm texting back that I can cover." She smiled sweetly and added, "And I'll treat you to free ice cream."

I raised my fist triumphantly. "Yes!"

When Grandma returned to the dining room, her expression was grim. "There's been a multiple-car accident. The hospital needs all the help it can get right now. I'm sorry, but I have to leave."

"Of course, Grandma," I said.

"Oh, my goodness. I hope everyone is okay," Mia murmured.

"So far, there have been no fatalities."

As she slipped into her hooded coat and wrapped a scarf around her neck, I asked, "You've got chains on your Explorer, right, Grandma?"

She patted my shoulder and reassured me. "Yes, Ethan, I'm all set for the weather, and I will drive carefully."

I opened the front door and peered into the dark sky. Thankfully, it wasn't snowing. "Text me when you get to the hospital."

"I will."

I watched her back the Explorer out of the garage from the hallway door. As the garage door slowly closed, I turned back to Mia. Gracie and Hank stood by her side. "Want to help me put leftovers in the fridge and clean up?"

"Let's do it."

***

After dinner, we settled into the living room to sit by the warmth of the electric fireplace. Inside the glass case, orange and yellow flames leaped and cast a mesmerizing glow in the room.

My cell phone chimed. "It's probably my grandma." I took out my phone and saw a text message from her.

The situation is dire—there are too many critical patients and not enough doctors. I'm afraid I won't be home until early tomorrow morning.

I'm so sorry, Grandma. You're the best, though, and I know you can help them.

Thank you, Ethan.

I put my phone down and looked at Mia. "My grandma won't be home until morning. Things are bad at the hospital."

"Oh no." Mia closed her eyes and said, "I'm sending prayers."

We sat in silence, gazing into the flickering blaze, both of us hoping for the survival of everyone affected. In the next moment, we snuggled closer together. Our lips met, igniting a wave of touching, caressing, and heavy breathing, the fire's warmth reflecting the heat building between us. Our eyes locked as we pulled apart to catch our breath.

Mia whispered, her breath warm against my skin, "Can I stay the night?"

I searched her eyes, and they were filled with an intense, animalistic hunger. Where did that come from? I had been to her place many times before, but we had never discussed the possibility of staying the night. Probably because we were never truly alone. Sarah and Glen were always checking in on Mia. But the thought of her spending the night with me and exploring each other's bodies sent a shiver down my spine. I imagined the softness of her skin against mine and the intoxicating scent that always surrounded her. If she were in my bed, I knew without a doubt that I would want to have sex with her.

"Ethan?"

After shaking off my thoughts, I responded, "Mia, I know you said that you've never had a boyfriend, but have you ever been intimate with a guy? Staying the night—that's a big step."

She pursed her lips, contemplating my question. "I'm sure I've been with a boy before because all this touching feels familiar, but my feelings for you are entirely different. With you, I feel a vulnerability I've never experienced with anyone else. It's as if I were meant to be with you."

Her admission sent a thrilling pulse racing through my veins. Heat spread within me as I imagined Mia pressed against me, my hands exploring her every curve while I softly kissed her. "Yes, I want you to stay the night with me."

I took her hand and led her down the hall to my bedroom. Thankfully, Hank and Gracie were asleep by the fireplace. My grandma wouldn't be home for hours, giving us plenty of privacy. I closed the bedroom door but left it slightly ajar, just in case Hank and Gracie woke up and wanted to come in.

Mia's gaze wandered around my bedroom, absorbing the posters on the walls and the world map hanging nearby. Her fingers traced the locations I had marked to visit. Then she spotted my guitar. "Do you play?"

"I played back in high school. This is my high school guitar."

She smiled, then turned her attention to my bookcase. "Wow, that's a lot of books. Have you read all of these?"

"Most of them. When I was younger and sicker, I couldn't do much, so reading became my pastime."

She approached me and wrapped her arms around me, whispering, "I don't want to talk anymore." After releasing me, she lay down on my bed.

Without hesitation, I joined her, lying on top of her and kissing her deeply as our tongues intertwined. My lips traced the curves of her body as I moved down from her neck to her breasts. Soft moans escaped her lips, urging me on. Our clothes came off, and we lay skin against skin, pressing our naked bodies together. When I touched her smooth skin, a wave of electricity ran through me. When she whispered my name, her warm breath made me want her even more.

She gasped as I slowly entered her, our bodies becoming one. Wrapping her legs around me, she pulled me deeper inside her, driving me insane. Together, we moved slowly at first and then urgently, thrusting faster and faster. Her breath came in quickened bursts, and her body trembled fervently as she cried out in ecstasy. I lost all control as she shuddered with her orgasm. Her passionate cries made my orgasm explode inside her. Our bodies shook for several minutes before we finally collapsed. We lay entwined in each other's arms, breathing heavily, our skin slick with sweat.

Mia's weeping echoed in my ears, and her warm tears touched my cheeks. I looked down to find her hiding her face in her hands and crying. Internally, I cringed. Had I made her cry? But why? Horrible memories from my past surfaced as I asked, "Mia, did I do something wrong?"

"It's just the opposite. I've just never been this happy before," she replied as a few more tears slipped down her cheeks.

Knowing her tears came from joy rather than sadness made me shudder with relief. Gently brushing her tears away, I embraced her tightly. "I'm happy, too," I said while stroking her hair.

At that moment, Gracie and Hank burst through the door, charging into my room. They immediately smothered us with wolf kisses, pressing their wet noses against our faces. Laughing, we ruffled their fur as they climbed all over us. After a few minutes, my wolves settled down at the foot of the bed. Hank curled up first, making a cozy nest out of the comforter, while Gracie nudged him with her paws before stretching out beside him.

Throwing on a pair of boxers, I got up and closed my bedroom door. I paused at my dresser to grab a T-shirt for Mia. I handed it to her and lay next to her and gazed at her beautiful body. She pulled the fabric over her head, allowing it to drape against her figure, and then she nestled beside me under the warm covers. I wrapped my arm around her, drawing her close. I whispered, "Good night, Mia."

"Good night, Ethan."

The gentle rise and fall of her chest lulled me into a peaceful sleep.

Chapter 6

My grandma got home from the hospital at 8:30 the next morning, and I had made eggs, crispy potatoes, and avocado toast for myself, Mia, and my grandma. After breakfast, Mia and I took Hank and Gracie for a walk. Thick, gray clouds filled the sky, suggesting that snowfall might be on the way. But for now, the sun peeked between the clouds, even though the air was crisp and cold. To me, it seemed like Hank and Gracie enjoyed the cold weather, the way they trotted along, wagging their tails and sniffing the air, or maybe it was the company around them.

As we walked along the path, the tree branches were covered in a thin layer of frost that sparkled in the soft morning light, and mist covered the tops of the mountains in the distance. Mia laced our fingers together and glanced up at me and said, "It was great to finally come over and visit you and your grandma at your house. I can't believe we've been hanging out for three months already!"

I squeezed her hand and replied, "I know. It feels like we've known each other forever."

"I know, right?"

We paused to share a kiss, but Hank and Gracie tugged on their leashes, pulling us forward and trotting down the path with their noses to the ground, eagerly investigating some scent.

***

Following our walk, I dropped off Mia at her cabin and then headed to my grandma's clinic to handle her books. Later that day, I'd have to return to Mia's and take her to work, but for now, I spent the rest of my morning reconciling my grandma's patients' accounts, reviewing charges, cross-checking insurance claims, and verifying payments. I made sure that Grandma never had to worry about that side of her business.

Millie knocked on my office door and asked, "Can you help with inventory? I've got Johnny working on it too, but with all the exam rooms full, I can't step away."

"Sure."

I joined Johnny in the supply room, picked up a hand scanner, and began scanning the barcodes. We quickly established a rhythm, dividing the shelves between us and alerting each other to any discrepancies we discovered. We double-checked each other's scans and cracked some dumb jokes to lighten the mood. Johnny's favorite was, "Why did the thermometer break up with the stethoscope? Because it couldn't handle the pressure." I liked, "What do you call a group of medical supplies that love to party? A Band-Aid." Jokes aside, we picked up the pace and felt relieved when we completed the tedious task, just in time for me to pick up Mia and take her to work.

When I arrived at her cabin, Mia stood outside, dressed in a maroon-colored uniform, complete with an apron decorated with colorful ice cream cones. I couldn't help but grin. "That's adorable."

She climbed into the passenger seat of my Jeep and playfully nudged my shoulder. "Knock it off."

"I'm serious. You look really cute."

She waved me off. "Whatever, let's go. I don't want to be late."

I chuckled and gave her a mock salute. "Yes, ma'am."

She giggled and leaned in to plant a kiss on my cheek.

With five minutes to spare, I pulled up in front of The Ice House and asked, "What time should I pick you up?"

"I've never worked a closing shift before. Can I text you when I'm ready?"

"Since it's a ten-minute drive, just text me ten minutes before you're ready."

"Sounds good."

Before Mia got out of the Jeep, I leaned over and kissed her softly. "Good luck with your shift," I murmured against her lips.

She smiled, her eyes sparkling as usual. "Thanks, Ethan. I'll text you later." After one last quick kiss, she hopped out of the Jeep and waved goodbye as she made her way inside.

I drove home, high on emotion. Mia was good for me, and I was incredibly happy about how things were progressing in our relationship, and maybe I was infatuated with her, but I truly believed it was the real thing. She made everything feel better, regardless of what it was, and I needed that in my life.

When I got home and walked into the house humming a tune, Hank and Gracie rushed over to greet me before darting off toward the kitchen. The delicious smells of ground beef and spicy tomato sauce wafted through the air, making my stomach growl. As I entered the kitchen, I saw my grandma stirring something in a large skillet. I approached her and peeked over her shoulder. "Sloppy joes! Nice, Grandma. We haven't had them since I was a kid."

"And homemade fries, too!"

"Can't wait! Do you need any help?"

"I think I've got it covered. Why don't you have a seat and tell me about your day?"

I grabbed a Coke from the fridge and settled down at the kitchen island. "It was pretty busy, and there was some boring stuff, like inventory. But now, I'm looking forward to relaxing until I have to leave and pick Mia up from work later tonight. How was your day?"

"It was busy too, especially after spending the night at the hospital and then having a full day of patients at the clinic. I'm ready for a relaxing evening and going to bed early."

"I bet." A thought occurred to me that Mia would need something for dinner, too. "Maybe I'll pack a to-go box for Mia to bring with me when I pick her up. I'm sure she'll want something for dinner instead of just ice cream."

"That's a sweet thought, Ethan."

"Grandma, how did you know Grandpa was the one?"

Her face brightened at the mention of his name. "When he arrived at our house on that old, rickety bicycle to deliver our newspaper, I knew he was the one."

"Really? So you didn't even know each other, and you knew?"

"That's right," she chuckled, stirring the hamburger in the skillet. "There was just something about his smile and the way he looked at me. I could see the kindness in his soul even back then." She glanced over at me. "Are you asking me about Grandpa because of something you're feeling for Mia?"

"Maybe," I confessed, a warmth creeping into my cheeks. "There's something about her, you know? I feel—I think I'm falling for her."

Grandma nodded, her eyes filled with understanding. "When someone touches your heart, that's how it all begins, Ethan."

"I believe she feels the same way about me."

"It's easy to see why she would. You're a lovely person."

"But you're my grandma; of course, you would feel that way."

She paused her cooking and stepped closer to me. "Ethan, you have a kind heart, and that's something anyone can see, not just your grandma."

Grandma's words always brought me back to reality and made me feel like a good person. "Thanks, Grandma," I said, inhaling the delicious aromas wafting from the kitchen. "Let's eat."

***

Mia texted me at 9:00 p.m. I quickly heated a sloppy joe and some fries, packing them into an insulated bag to take with me. I left a note for my grandma next to the coffee maker. She had already gone to bed. After the night at the hospital and then working in the clinic, she was exhausted.

Hank and Gracie followed me toward the garage, their tails wagging. I shook my head. "Not this time, guys." I gave them each a scratch behind their ears. "I'll be back later." They tilted their heads, staring at me as I closed the door behind me. I stared at the door for a brief moment and got into my Jeep and headed to The Ice House.

Ten minutes later, I pulled into a parking spot by the front door. Most of the shops had closed for the night, which left the street almost empty except for a few parked cars, so I had my choice of parking spots. Taking the bag of food with me, I stepped into the chilly night. A gust of wind blew open my jacket, and I ran toward the front door. Mia held open the door, and I dashed inside.

The ice cream shop felt warm and inviting. Vintage posters of ice cream cones decorated the pastel-colored walls, creating a cheerful atmosphere. Behind the glass counter, various colors and mouthwatering ice cream flavors were on display. I placed the bag on one of the small round tables and pulled out the food. "I thought you might enjoy dinner."

She held out a waffle cone filled with rich chocolate and creamy vanilla ice cream. "Thank you! I'd love that. And here's your ice cream cone, just as I promised."

The two of us sat at the table, with her eagerly biting into the sloppy joe while I gorged on my ice cream.

Mia let out a satisfied moan, "This is so good."

"I can't take credit. Grandma made dinner, and it was super tasty, but so is this ice cream." I leaned in and kissed her cheek. "Thank you."

She blew me a kiss before returning to her sloppy joe, occasionally popping fries into her mouth.

"So, how was the closing shift?"

Between bites, she replied, "I'm sticking to days. Everyone gathered here after the movie theater let out, and I served them all by myself."

She fluttered her eyelashes at me and added, "But now, I'm with you, and that makes it all better."

"Aw. How sweet. My day was pretty busy, but not as hectic as yours." I wondered if she wanted to go straight home or come back to my place. Hopefully, she would be up for hanging out together, whether at her place or mine. "So, am I taking you home, or should we head to my place?"

"Let's make it a cozy night at my place. I want to change into something comfy."

"That sounds like a plan."

I popped the end of the ice cream cone into my mouth while she finished her last bite of her sloppy joe. "Is there anything else you need to take care of before closing?"

"The ice cream tubs need to be put in the freezer, and then we just have to turn off the lights and lock up."

"I can help with that."

"Thanks. Let me show you where the ice cream tubs go."

We finished putting everything away in just five minutes. With the store keys in her hand, she turned off the lights before we stepped out the front door. As she turned the key in the lock, a male voice called out from behind us, "Asthma Boy! I can't believe it. How long has it been?"

The tiny hairs on the back of my neck prickled as I recognized the voice—Wally, the bully from high school. Memories of his relentless taunts flooded back, and I forced a smile, trying to mask the nervous flutter in my stomach. I slowly turned to face him, and he wasn't alone. His sidekick, Randy, stood beside him, wearing a smirk that mirrored the arrogance I remembered. Wally had put on weight since high school, and not fat, but muscle. His once lanky frame now looked pretty intimidating, but Randy was still short and stocky, sporting a buzz cut with a tattoo on his forearm.

Mia picked up on my tension and instinctively moved closer to me. Her eyes narrowed as she shifted her gaze between Randy and Wally, then back to me. I nudged her slightly, urging her forward. "Just ignore them."

"What? No hello?" Wally shouted, his tone mocking. "Aren't you happy to see me?"

I kept walking, but Mia turned around and demanded, "Who are you, and what do you want?"

Randy's laughter echoed in the air. "Did you finally manage to get a girlfriend, Asthma Boy?"

When I didn't respond or turn around, a fist struck me between the shoulder blades. The blow sent a sharp jolt of pain through my spine, knocking the wind out of me and lurching me forward a few steps. Fear washed over me as I experienced that all-too-familiar sensation of struggling to breathe. Mia grabbed my arm to steady me, but her eyes remained fixed on Wally and Randy. Wally dealt another blow, landing in my gut and forcing air from my lungs. The impact pushed me to the ground, gasping and clutching my chest. The punches hit like a sledgehammer, sending sharp pain coursing through my ribcage. My vision blurred as I tried to fill my lungs, but it was like breathing through a thin straw. My wheezing echoed in my ears, sending a wave of panic through me. I grabbed my inhaler out of my pocket, but Randy kicked it from my hand. It slid onto the sidewalk just as Wally's boot came crashing down on it, shattering the inhaler under his weight.

The wild laughter boomed around me, mingling with their taunts, "Can't catch your breath, Asthma Boy?"

Mia's eyes widened in horror as she witnessed these two bullies cripple me and take away my lifeline. Her hands clenched into fists, and her face flushed with rage. She stepped forward, her voice firm and unwavering. "You need to stop this now or you'll regret it."

Randy sneered, "What are you going to do about it, girlie?"

Mia stood tall, electricity crackling around her as her demeanor shifted. The turquoise color of her eyes transformed into a chilling, inhuman gold, while an unseen breeze lifted her hair. Her fingers elongated into claws, and her lips curled back to reveal lethal fangs glistening with saliva. A low growl escaped her throat. "I warned you."

In a panic, I crawled toward my Jeep and ducked behind a wheel, my gaze darting toward this new Mia.

Randy and Wally stumbled backward, their eyes wide with terror as they scrambled to put distance between themselves and the supernatural creature. Sheer terror replaced their confidence. "Get away from us, you freak!" Wally yelled over his shoulder as the two cowards raced down the street, hopped into a car, and sped away.

Leaning against my Jeep, gasping for air, fear and shock crushed my lungs, and I was only getting worse. *What the hell just happened? Had Mia really turned into some sort of wolf-like thing? Her strength was insane, but maybe my eyes were playing tricks on me?* The haunting images lingered in my head as I teetered between consciousness and unconsciousness, desperately fighting to breathe.

Mia knelt beside me, her hand resting gently on my shoulder. When I looked up at her, she was Mia again—the terrifying creature had vanished. Confusion washed over me as my body began to collapse. Mia, whom I thought I knew, felt like a stranger again, yet I felt compelled to understand what had happened to her, even as my asthma was suffocating me.

"Ethan, focus on me." She moved her hand from my shoulder to my chest, her touch warm and soothing. "Just breathe. Do you have an extra inhaler?"

Every breath I took felt like an assault on my body. A new fear—dying—gripped me more than Mia's wolf thing. My life hinged on getting air! Helpless and exposed, I stared at her, paralyzed by my struggle for oxygen. I pointed to the passenger seat of my Jeep, silently hoping she would understand that I needed her to check the glove compartment for a spare inhaler.

She glanced at my Jeep before turning her attention back on me. After a moment's hesitation, she reached into my jeans pocket, retrieving my keys and clicking the remote. In a frantic rush, she opened the passenger door and began searching through the glove compartment.

"There's nothing there!" Her voice mirrored the frantic pounding in my chest. Her eyes darted along the street, as if searching for an answer. "I have one!" she shouted. "An extra inhaler is in my bathroom medicine cabinet."

My only response was a raspy breath escaping my lips.

She effortlessly lifted me into the passenger seat of my Jeep. I couldn't comprehend how she managed to lift me, a 165-pound guy, as if I weighed nothing at all. Had some hidden power awakened within her after she turned into a wolf-like creature? The strength she exhibited shattered everything I thought I knew about her. Questions popped into my head, and I knew I should ask, but not now, later. I had to breathe first.

She took a deep breath before she started the Jeep and then focused on the street. *Wait?* I thought she'd never driven before, but she easily maneuvered my Jeep up the winding road toward her cabin. I believed her mission was to reach her cabin before I lost consciousness. But how was she driving like a professional and didn't have a driver's license? Was that another thing she hadn't remembered but suddenly returned to her? Was any of this really happening? Had I actually passed out, and was this all in my head, like a crazy dream? The sensation of the seat beneath me felt too vivid to be a feverish hallucination. Was this bizarre reality merely a figment of my oxygen-starved imagination?

My Jeep suddenly stopped, and Mia jumped out and ran to the passenger side. She picked me up and carried me into her cabin. She laid me on the sofa and took off down the hall. Moments later, she returned with an inhaler. She positioned the device between my lips and pressed it twice, releasing medication into my mouth.

More raspy breaths escaped me as she pulled my shirt up and pressed her warm hands against my bare skin. "Breathe," she urged again.

The warmth of her hands and the medication helped ease the tightness in my lungs, letting me draw deeper breaths. Yet, I still couldn't stop my body from shaking, nor could I control the sweat covering my skin. "I can't stop shaking, and I feel sick."

"I think you're having a panic attack." Mia snatched the wool blanket from the sofa, draped it around my shoulders, and gently rubbed my back. "Take slow, deep breaths. You're safe."

"Was I safe?" I thought as I inhaled and exhaled several times. My shaking lessened, and my body began to feel normal, but my mind was reeling from the images of her eyes shifting colors, sharp fangs emerging from her mouth, and deadly claws replacing fingernails. Had my eyes played tricks on me? Had I imagined it? No, I saw it, and so did Wally and Randy, but the question I had was what had I seen? I turned to face her and stammered, "W-what are you?"

She blinked several times, and then her eyes opened wide. "I'm human."

Slowly, I shook my head. "No human could do what I just saw, and honestly, I would have bolted out that door by now if I wasn't sitting here trying to recover from a severe asthma attack."

Her shoulders fell, and her confidence shattered like fragile glass. Tears glistened in her eyes. "I would never hurt you, Ethan."

"Earlier today I'd have no problem believing that. Now...I just don't know what to believe. You never said anything about this, this—I don't even know what to call it—and that," I gestured to all of her, "should have been something you would have told me."

Everything between us grew tense. She sat stiffly next to me, staring straight ahead. Her hands brushed her tears away, and then she faced me. "I understand why you're saying all of that." Her gaze shifted to the floor. "There are things that I've kept hidden from you."

With a hint of sarcasm, I asked, "Like how you can effortlessly lift a guy who weighs 165 pounds or handle a four-wheel-drive Jeep like a pro?"

She met my eyes, hers were now dry. Her hands were clutched in her lap, and remorse radiated off her as she said, "It's going to be hard to share what I have to say." She remained quiet for a few seconds before continuing. "I've been open about several things in my life, being homeless, that I never knew my parents, that I never had a boyfriend, and whether I have any family.

"When I was very young, some homeless people found me. I don't remember being left on the streets, but that's where they found me and took me to their makeshift shelter. They cared for me as one of their own, and I became part of their family. Three years later, people dressed in black and hiding their faces behind masks invaded our camp. It was chaos. People were running anywhere to get away, but these masked individuals managed to capture eight of us, herding us into a van. They locked us inside and drove away. The journey felt endless, and the eight of us huddled together, terrified, not knowing what was going on.

"They took us to an abandoned warehouse. The building looked cold and intimidating, and I didn't want to go inside. There were many others like us sitting on the cement floor of the building. I counted thirty frightened faces staring back at us. Our abductors dropped us off like garbage, handing us over to a new group of masked people dressed in military gear. They blindfolded us and injected us with something. It made me feel dizzy and sick. I couldn't keep my eyes open, and everything went dark."

Her eyes were unreadable and distant as she recounted her unbelievable story, but her voice sounded so calm. Had she detached herself from the emotions tied to those memories? As I listened, I continued to doubt whether any of this was real, but because it was so far removed from reality, I considered that maybe it was true.

"I awoke alone."

Her voice pulled me out of my thoughts, and I directed my attention to her once more.

"Isolated from the others, I was lying on a hospital bed wearing a hospital gown, with an IV

in my arm, and I was surrounded by medical equipment. A horrible smell, like antiseptic, reeked inside the all-white room. In the corner of the room a door stood slightly ajar, and inside was a small bathroom. Next to the bed, a monitor beeping rapidly displayed my racing heart. The whole vibe of the room made me panic. I had to get out of there, but when I tried to move, a sharp pain shot through my whole body. My scream echoed in the room.

"A person in green scrubs and a mask entered without saying a word. They approached my IV and injected something into it. Instantly, the room began to blur, and darkness enveloped me once more."

I couldn't believe what I was hearing. What the hell had happened to her? I couldn't stay silent, despite her wanting me to. "This really happened to you? It sounds more like a scene from a movie than something in real life."

"Yes, of course it did!" She glared at me, seemingly irked that I doubted her.

Pain clouded the brightness of her eyes, and I could see how badly she wanted—no, needed—me to believe her. It was just so out there, but something deep down inside me already believed, I think. "The look in your eyes tells me you're not making this up. Please, continue."

Again, she stared off in the distance before bringing her focus back to me. "I can't go over every detail. It's too painful, but I'll tell you as much as I can, okay?" She paused, glancing at me, as if anticipating my reaction.

"Okay."

"I was eight when I arrived at that place, and I escaped eleven years later. It wasn't a hospital; it was a military black site called DFOG—Defense Forces of Genesis." She clenched her jaw, forcing the words out. "I was one of thirty-eight homeless people they experimented on."

"What?" I gasped, my breath catching in my throat—not from asthma but from sheer shock.

"They needed subjects that no one would miss. Who better than a homeless person to experiment on? We were expendable. They tortured and abused us all because DFOG wanted super soldiers. They injected us over and over again with wolf DNA. We were physically and mentally scarred, and six people lost their lives.

"But they got what they wanted. Intelligent, adaptable, courageous, strong, heightened senses, and soldiers who had the ability to heal themselves."

Listening to her, I sat overwhelmed. How could I respond to any of it? That kind of stuff didn't happen in the real world, or at least not in mine. If I hadn't seen her transform into that wolf creature, I would have thought she was crazy and would never have believed her. What freaked me out the most was she spent eleven years of her life there. I couldn't comprehend that, and how had she managed to escape a black site? I desperately wanted to know more.

"I can't even believe all that happened to you and the others or that humans did this to other humans. It's appalling, barbaric, and inhumane. Simply saying, 'I'm sorry,' isn't enough, but I am truly sorry." Without letting her respond, I fired off, "Did they experiment on you for eleven years? Was that the time frame to complete the transition? How did you manage to escape? The security had to be over the top."

Sadness pulled at the corners of her mouth, her memories appearing to dredge up old emotions. "It did not take eleven years. The injections were administered in phases to monitor our responses, and they were excruciating. Our bodies fought against this foreign DNA. People suffered from hunched backs, lost their ability to speak, and grew pointed ears and fur patches across their bodies. In their attempts to play God, they didn't think of the consequences.

"As time passed, they adjusted the genetics to achieve our supernatural gifts and at the same time, minimize the defects the injection caused. Though, from what I saw, I think all the versions were to eliminate us having any resemblance to a wolf. Though, they were unable to achieve that goal and had to settle on us having fangs, claws, and shifting eye colors."

She paused and narrowed her eyes on me. "You seem to be breathing easier, and you're not as pale. Are you feeling better?"

I had been so engrossed in her story that I completely forgot about my asthma attack. The chills had subsided, and the tightness in my chest was gone. I took a deep breath, demonstrating my improvement. "Much better."

"Good." She pointed toward the kitchen. "I'm going to grab a bottled water. Would you like one?"

"Sure. Thanks."

Returning with two bottles of water, she settled in closer to me and handed me one. She finished about a quarter of her bottle before continuing. "At 14, I had completed the transformation. That was the beginning of my super soldier journey. Our captain pushed us physically and mentally. None of us had any knowledge of what we were training on: neutralizing threats, handling weapons, rescue missions, destroying targets, and survival skills, just to name a few. They wanted us ready for missions that regular soldiers couldn't handle."

My jaw dropped in disbelief. "What? Wait a minute. Are you saying you were part of a covert super soldier unit? That's, like, incredible."

"No, it wasn't incredible. We were prisoners," she snapped. "It was a nightmare. I was just 14 years old, not mentally prepared to handle any of that. I was a test subject, a part-human, part-animal creature stripped of my normal life."

Recognizing the hurt in her voice, a wave of regret washed over me. I had a habit of blurting out my thoughts. Hearing "super soldier" triggered an obsession I had when I was younger. A TV show called Super Soldiers was my all-time favorite. I was glued to the TV screen whenever it came on. I thought they were the coolest and most badass supernatural beings I'd ever seen. I wanted to become one, but all of that changed as I grew older and learned they were fictional characters, or so I thought. I had to apologize. Using my most sincere tone, I said, "I'm sorry, Mia. I didn't mean to be insensitive or make light of what you went through." Trying to lighten the mood, I added, "Besides, speaking my mind was one of the things you liked about me, right?"

Her eyes narrowed as she crossed her arms and just stared at me. Clearly unimpressed. The silence grew, as did her displeasure with me. I knew I needed to say something. "Mia, I am truly sorry. Please continue. I want to hear," I put my hand over my heart, "and feel everything you've been through. I swear I won't interrupt you again. I promise."

Mia hesitated, searching my eyes for a few seconds. I smiled, hoping my expression conveyed my sincerity. Something must have clicked as she uncrossed her arms and continued. "Two years later, I was assigned to a team that focused on high-risk targets and recovering sensitive information. During one mission, we breached our target's command center and planted spyware to copy their computers' digital files. I was tasked with collecting data using an encrypted device. While the data was uploading, I stumbled on a DFOG personnel file on the target's computer. As the information scrolled across the screen, my heart raced at the sight of a familiar name and what followed, their emergency contact details: a name, phone number, and address. I repeated their information in my head over and over again, memorizing it. Glancing over my shoulder, I made sure no one was close enough to see what I saw. This file was my leverage. Personal information about DFOG was a powerful weapon in a world where I was completely powerless. With this information I could take back control.

"After the upload was complete, I handed the device to my captain. That night, I began to plot my escape."

I was thoroughly engaged, like I was in the middle of her mission with her, and I remained silent as promised, but questions swirled in my mind. Why did DFOG exist in the first place? Was there really a need for these super soldiers with wolf-like traits? Could these soldiers control the beast inside them? Was Mia a threat to me? No, I didn't believe that. I had never encountered a more kindhearted person, but I pinched myself to make sure I wasn't dreaming. In the world I lived in, superhumans didn't exist, at least not before I witnessed it happen. That was proof.

"Accessing the DFOG's floor plan was out of the question," Mia explained, "but my duties let me go through the building without drawing attention. I observed the guards' routines, noted their shift changes, memorized the layout of security checkpoints, and identified blind spots in the surveillance cameras, making a mental map of everything." She sighed heavily. "But I was just one person, with or without supernatural powers. The security was too tight, and the risk of me being caught was too high. It became obvious that I would not be able to escape. My carefully thought-out plan fell apart."

"But here you are," I pointed out. "Did someone help you, or did you find another way?"

Her shoulders sank as if the weight of her past was resting on them. "I did find another, or should I say it found me. It was all pure luck. A terrorist group had seized control of a hospital, and they were demanding a ransom for the patients they held as hostages inside. Our mission was to rescue the hostages.

"Things rapidly spiraled out of control once we infiltrated the hospital. The terrorists were far more organized than we anticipated, and the scene became chaotic. Gunshots ripped through the hall, and my teammates fell one after another, making a sickening thud as their bodies hit the ground and turning the hospital floor into a sea of red blood.

"I ducked inside the hospital supply room, taking cover, and quickly discarded my tactical gear and slipped into a patient gown. Using a scalpel, I cut into my leg and removed the DFOG tracker. The sight of the blood-soaked hospital gown would help me blend in as one of the patients and hopefully spare my life. After bandaging my leg, I cautiously exited the supply room and merged with the other patients and critically wounded civilians in the corridor.

"The negotiator's voice came over the loudspeakers, saying they would pay part of the ransom to the terrorists if they released some of the patients, especially the critical ones. The terrorists must have agreed, as they grabbed several patients, including me, and herded us toward the entrance. With my hands trembling, I walked out the doors and staggered into the street with several other patients. My heart pounded in my chest as I stepped back slowly, retreating further into the street and putting distance between me and the hospital.

"The sound of a train echoed to my right. Without hesitation, I dashed toward it with wolf speed. A freight train thundered down the tracks, its cargo containers banging together like a rolling fortress. The door of one container was partially open, revealing stacks of hay bales inside.

The door was cracked open just large enough for me to slip inside. Using every ounce of strength in my body, I raced alongside the train and jumped. My claws latched onto the edge of the door, and I pulled myself inside, tumbling onto the hay. I lay there, breathless and grateful. This train was taking me away from the horrors I had faced for eleven long years."

Compassion filled me as I looked into her eyes, reflecting both sadness and strength, and I hugged her. She had been through so much pain. "I'm so sorry." I knew that wasn't much, but I didn't know what else to say.

Her body relaxed, and her arms came around me, as if the weight of her struggles had lifted. We sat quietly on the sofa, holding each other for a while before she eventually broke away and continued.

"When I awoke, the light of dawn filtered through the cracked container door, shining over the hay. My surroundings jolted me back to reality and reminded me that I had escaped. The name and address I had memorized flooded into my head. My only thought was to find this person.

"Looking out of the container door, I noticed the mountains rising beyond a freight depot. The train began to slow and came to a stop outside the depot. This was my chance. I stepped out of the container and into the small mountain town. Metal tracks and wooden platforms wrapped around the vacant depot. There were trees everywhere, and I remember the cool morning air smelled like pine, distracting me for a moment.

"Hoping to find a sign indicating my location, I scanned the area, but I didn't see anything that told me where I was. The thin fabric of my hospital gown wasn't much protection from the cold air. I couldn't stop shivering, and I knew I needed warmth to survive. I needed shoes and clothes, but without any money, that was a long shot.

"Snow began to fall as I made my way down the mountain. I desperately needed to find shelter. My feet were cut and bleeding when I came across an opening to a cave. This might sound silly, but I felt like it was a sign from God granting me shelter, so I entered. The cave kept out the weather somewhat, but it was still very cold, and the weather was getting worse. To stay warm, I curled up into a ball and held my legs close to my chest. My fingers had grown numb, and I couldn't keep my teeth from chattering. My eyelids grew heavier, and my mind started to wander when a comforting sense of drowsiness replaced my shaking, pulling me into a dreamlike state.

"The next time I opened my eyes, I was in your grandmother's clinic."

My heart ached for her. She had come close to losing everything. Surviving such a harrowing experience, and alone, showed how strong she was. I would do everything in my power to make sure she never had to go through anything like that ever again.

She placed her hand over mine as she said, "There are things that I know now that I didn't understand back then. What I'm about to tell you is the hardest thing I've ever had to say."

My head jerked backward, and I stared at her. "Oh, my God! What could possibly be worse than everything you've already said?"

Her hand trembled, and her lips parted slightly, yet no sound came out. It was as though she was wrestling with whatever she was about to tell me.

I squeezed her hand gently, hoping to calm her nerves. "Whatever it is, you can tell me."

Taking a deep breath and then letting it out, she began, "I believe God was with me on that day we entered the hospital. He allowed me to escape death and sent that train to me to take me to Doford Peaks. That was the very place I was searching for, and the person I wanted to find, Dr. Evelyn Porter."

My mouth went dry and blood rushed to my head as the room spun around me. Single words ran through my brain: impossible, coincidence, Grandma, DFOG. Little by little, the shock lessened and my thoughts became coherent again. The thought that God had guided her to Doford Peaks and to my grandma felt almost too incredible to grasp. I needed answers. "Why Doford Peaks? And why my grandma?"

She swallowed hard. "Okay, just listen. Dr. Garrison Porter listed her as his emergency contact, and I assumed Evelyn was his wife. I thought she might be someone who could reason with him and stop his involvement in DFOG. She led me to Doford Peaks."

The moment I heard her mention my dad's name, a sickeningly cold feeling swept over me. But my dad had never served in the military, at least not to my knowledge. And what about my mom? They were supposed to be working together on a cure for asthma. Mia hadn't brought up my mom. Were they involved in the wolf-like super soldier thing? Was that their plan to cure asthma by manipulating DNA? I tried to shake off the thought. I couldn't believe my dad or mom would be part of something so malicious. They were assholes, but not crazy assholes. I found myself grappling with the unsettling possibility that both of them might be involved in this whole mess. I had to ask about my mom. I had to find out if she was involved. I cleared my throat, then hesitantly asked, "You mentioned someone in green scrubs. Were there other doctors at DFOG?"

"Yes, many. The medical department was fully staffed with researchers, physicians, and surgeons."

"Do you know their names?"

"Just the ones that treated me."

"And?"

"Dr. Porter and Dr. Owen led the research team. Dr. Collins gave me my injections and watched me for side effects. There's one other doctor I heard about from the other soldiers, Dr. Fowler. He led the surgical team."

Her statement was so matter-of-fact without any emotion, but she confirmed my suspicions that both my parents were involved. The more it sank in, the more it wounded me. The ground suddenly was ripped out from beneath me. Betrayal, anger, and grief swelled within me, and my lungs tightened like a vise, draining every last bit of air from my body. It hurt to breathe. My vision was blurry, and I slumped forward.

"Ethan!" Mia shouted in panic and lunged for the inhaler resting on the coffee table and pressed it between my lips, pushing down on the device. With her other hand spread across my chest, she urged, "Breathe."

With each passing breath, the constriction lessened, allowing air into my lungs. The room came back into focus, and the pain in my ribs was gone, but my heart still ached for Mia and the others who had suffered. My parents had once again screwed up someone's life, and their actions weighed heavily on me. Just as Mia had confessed to me, I needed to do the same for her. I glanced away from her as I admitted, "This is all my fault. I'm responsible for what happened to you and the others."

She placed her hand on my knee and asked, "What do you mean? How can you be responsible for this?"

I cringed inside as I envisioned people mutilated by those injections. "Dr. Porter and Dr. Owen are my parents. They're trying to 'cure' me."

Sucking in a deep breath, her eyes widened, clearly taken aback. I could see the thoughts racing through her mind as she began to piece everything together. Her expression softened, and she gently rested her hand on my knee. "Ethan, you can't hold yourself responsible for their actions. I know this is all very overwhelming and unbelievable, but I promise we'll get through this together."

A flood of emotions erupted from my soul, fueled by my parents' abandonment, lies, excuses, and blame. I was an experiment too rather than a son—invisible and forgotten. Every missed birthday and every forgotten promise left a void where love should have been. I sagged against her, and she held me close and cried.

We fed off each other's pain, but the warmth of our embrace started to ease both of our suffering. I kissed her gently, savoring the sweetness of her lips, hoping to express how much I cared and how sorry I was. My trust, respect, and affection for Mia deepened as if we had been together for years instead of months, despite the fact that she was some sort of hybrid human creature. I couldn't explain why that part of her didn't matter to me, but it didn't. All I knew was that my heart wanted her, and I had no control over it, but if I had, I'd still want to be with her. She saved my life and me, but did I have the courage to say it? *Was there a dummies guide to how to date? Were there steps to follow? Was it too soon to say anything? The last thing I want to do is scare her off with something I said.* I was torn between the fear of overwhelming her and the desire to be honest about how I felt. The idea of not saying something was equally daunting. I didn't know how I should proceed—confess or keep my feelings to myself.

"Ethan, where do we go from here?" Her voice cut through my thoughts. "Those guys saw my wolf side."

"They're spineless jerks," I said, feeling a rush of confidence as I locked eyes with hers. "Sure, they're bullies, but deep down, they're cowards. There's no way they'll say anything for fear of being laughed at." I stood up and extended my hand. "What we are going to do is talk to my grandma. My dad's involved, and he's her son."

Her eyes widened, and she sat frozen on the sofa. "She won't believe me."

I furrowed my brows and tilted my head. "But she's the reason you came here. Why don't you want to talk to her now?"

She swallowed and clasped her hands in her lap. "I lived in captivity for so long, and it was so normal to me, but to an outsider, I wasn't sure. At your grandma's clinic, when I woke up, I was back in the real world where hybrids and super soldiers didn't exist. When Sheriff Reid showed up and said those things about database searches, I got scared. I didn't want to be captured by DFOG again, so I just couldn't bring myself to say anything, and the longer I remained silent, the easier it became to forget my past. No matter how much I wanted to help the other soldiers, I thought of myself first." She hung her head. "I know that was wrong."

"Don't beat yourself up. Anyone in your shoes would have done the same thing." Her wolf form flashed in my mind—those golden eyes, sharp fangs, and long claws. "I think I know a way that my grandma will believe you. Can you shift into your, um, wolf side whenever you want?"

She nodded.

"If you shift, she'll believe you. Plus, all the effort you put into reaching Doford Peaks won't be wasted." I glanced at my smartwatch. "I can't believe it's midnight already. Do you have to work tomorrow?"

"Since I worked tonight, I'm off tomorrow."

"Spend the night with me. We can talk to my grandma tonight without worrying about the time, and I'll make you breakfast in the morning."

A soft giggle escaped her lips, and she flashed a sweet smile. "Let me change out of this uniform and grab an overnight bag." She pressed a quick kiss on my lips before dashing off to her room.

CHAPTER 7

Hank and Gracie rushed toward Mia and me, howling as soon as we stepped inside my house. We greeted them by stroking their heads and scratching behind their ears. Watching my wolves interact with Mia, everything suddenly made sense. That winter morning, they had sensed her injuries, recognizing her as one of their own. They had picked up on her scent and instinctively knew she was in danger. That was what drove their urgency—why they had pulled my grandma and me toward her so desperately. They needed to save a member of their pack. Now, I understand the depth of their bond with her and why Hank was so loyal. She was part of their world—the wolf world—a true member of the pack.

Noises coming from the kitchen drifted into the hallway, leading us in that direction. My grandma was pouring herself a cup of coffee at 12:30 in the morning! Not the best option if you want to fall asleep. "Hey, Grandma," I said, swallowing a lump in my throat as I braced myself for the bombshell Mia and I were about to drop.

Her eyes narrowed in suspicion as she stared at me. Placing her hand on her hip, she waved me forward. "Ethan Jared Porter, I know you all too well. What's going on?"

Mia's tight-lipped expression reflected my anxiety. I gestured toward the chairs around the kitchen island. "Grandma, you really should sit down."

She stood her ground, arms crossed. "Tell me, Ethan."

"Um." I paused, my mind racing to find the right words for something so unbelievable. The tension rose the more I remained silent, and I was well aware of Grandma's gaze fixed on me. My heart raced as I still struggled with my choice of words, but I had to say something. "Well," I began, taking a deep breath, "there's this secret government that's creating enhanced soldiers using wolf DNA." My throat went dry as I blurted out, "Mom and Dad are leading the experiment. They made Mia into one!"

A skeptical smile crept onto her face as her eyebrows shot upward. She shook her head slightly, attempting to grasp the absurdity of my statement. "Ethan, are you kidding me?"

Mia transformed before I could respond. Her golden eyes locked onto my grandma as she bared her fangs and slashed her claws through the air, instantly wiping the smile off my grandma's face. My grandma stood still, her mouth open, as the coffee mug slipped from her hands and shattered on the floor. Within seconds, she bolted out of the kitchen, brushing against my shoulder as she sped past.

Mia quickly reverted to her human form, tears welling in her eyes. I placed my hand on her shoulder. "It's okay."

Just then, my grandma shouted, "I knew it!"

We rushed out of the kitchen and found my grandma in her office, seated behind her desk with her laptop open, her eyes wide. Her gaze shifted from the screen to us. "I knew it!" she declared again. "Mia's red blood cells were smaller, more uniform, and contained a higher potassium concentration. What I thought I observed that day was an abnormality, but what I was really looking at was an extraordinary composition of both human and animal blood, confirming that Mia is not entirely human."

"I'm sorry, it's true," Mia admitted. "But I never intended to deceive you or Ethan."

Grandma was missing the most important fact: my parents. "Grandma, did you not hear what I said? Mom and Dad are responsible!" Anger churned in my stomach as I raised my voice. "This is their fault! Mia isn't the only one. There are others—abducted, stripped of their rights, and forced to be test subjects in this insane experiment. And how did Mom and Dad get involved with the military? We need to do something. We have to end this!"

My grandma's face turned pale as she grasped the full picture. "Are you sure, Ethan? I can't believe that they would be involved in something so heinous."

I looked at Mia and gestured with my hand in a circular motion. "Can you please fill in my grandma?"

"Well," Mia cleared her throat and slightly raised her voice. "I was living in a homeless camp when I, along with eight others, was abducted. We were taken to Defense Forces of Genesis, DFOG, a secret military black site, held captive, and used as test subjects. For years, we were treated like lab rats to perfect their experiment. Some were left mutilated, and others died.

"After the injections were complete, they had their super soldiers and sent us on missions. That's when I came across your information. Dr. Porter listed you as his emergency contact. I managed to escape several months later, and during that mission where I escaped, terrorists murdered the rest of my team. I traveled all this way looking for you, hoping you could help us, as there are still other captives at the military base."

"Mom's involved in this scheme too," I said bitterly. "She and Dad are conspiring with the military to create these 'super soldiers.' This is what they've been doing all these years, making soldiers, not a cure for asthma, as they preached to us. They lied to us, Grandma!"

My grandma sat motionless, a deep frown creasing her forehead. She stared straight ahead, not saying a word as her breath caught and she clutched the edge of the table. In disbelief, she whispered, "Dear God." Then her gaze turned to Mia. "What was the name of the military?"

"Defense Forces of Genesis, though they refer to themselves as DFOG." Mia paused for a moment, her brows coming together, and then shook her head. "I have no idea how long these experiments have been going on, but I spent eleven years there before I escaped."

Grandma gasped, and her shoulders slumped forward. It was as if Mia's words had physically pushed her back into her chair, visibly shaken. "I am so sorry, Mia. To have endured all of that for eleven years is unbelievable. I can't imagine what you must have gone through, and for my son to keep his involvement from me. I'm speechless."

My face flushed and I clenched my fists. "And they kept it from me, too! Always giving me the guilt trip about trying to cure my asthma. We should call Mom and Dad, confront them, and demand that they free their prisoners."

Grandma sat upright and waved her hand in a dismissive fashion. "No. I need to talk to Sheriff Reid first. This situation is much bigger than both of us. He has connections with the FBI, but it's almost 1:30 in the morning. We'll have to wait a bit, but for now, we can all use some sleep to clear our minds."

"I'm feeling pretty drained," Mia admitted, wrapping her arms around herself and stifling a yawn. "I left my bag in the kitchen, so I'll go grab it."

The moment Mia stepped out, I let out a sigh and turned to my grandma. "When I picked up Mia from work, we ran into Wally and Randy, if you can believe it. They haven't changed. They're still the same old bullies from school, and they didn't hesitate to punch me a couple of times again. It triggered a bad asthma episode, and Wally smashed my inhaler. That's when, out of nowhere, Mia turns into this wolf-like thing and defends me. At that moment, I didn't know what was scarier, her or Wally and Randy, and she freaked them out too and they ran away. She just picked me up like I weighed nothing and put me in the Jeep. She handed me an extra inhaler at her place, and that's when she told me everything. What's weird is that I should be freaked out about the whole thing, but," I shrugged, lifting my palms, "I'm not. She's just Mia to me."

My grandma held me in her arms in a tight embrace as she murmured, "I'm so sorry this happened to you, Ethan. I'm glad Mia was there to defend you. I also can't believe the suffering this poor girl has endured because of our family. We have to find a way to make amends."

****

The next morning, Mia and I sat together in the living room, basking in the warmth of the electric fireplace. Hank and Gracie lay stretched out in front of it. Sunlight streamed through the large windows, adding to the warmth. The smell of coffee wafted in from the kitchen, but I'd already had three cups, waiting for Sheriff Reid to show up. He was supposed to be here at 9:00 a.m. It was already 9:10 a.m. He was late. The more I looked at my smartwatch, the more my anxiety rose. What was taking him so long? On the other hand, he might not believe Mia and totally blow us off, so I was worried about that too. Her story was challenging to grasp, and this would be my third time hearing it. My wildest dreams did not include living in a time where genetic editing was a reality or that my parents and the military were the instigators.

Footsteps approaching the living room pulled me from my thoughts, and I met Sheriff Reid's gaze as he entered with my grandma. He tipped his hat and said, "Ethan, Mia."

We greeted him with a simultaneous, "Hello."

Grandma motioned to one of the armchairs. "Sheriff Reid, please take a seat. Would you like some coffee or tea?"

He shook his head. "No, thank you. I've had more cups than I can count this morning."

"That was like my morning waiting for you," I thought.

Grandma settled into the opposite armchair and got straight to the point. "I asked you here because we have some new information about Mia's past, and I need your assistance."

He raised his eyebrows in surprise. "New information."

Grandma sighed before continuing. "There's a military organization known as the Defense Forces of Genesis, but it appears their initials are what's used, DFOG. They have been abducting young individuals and conducting DNA-altering experiments on them for years and without their consent. Many endured severe physical mutations, and some did not survive." She paused and then stated, "Their goal is to create hybrid human-wolf super soldiers."

I kept my eyes on Sheriff Reid. He shifted uncomfortably in his chair, tapping his fingers against the armrest. His eyes flitted between Mia, me, and Grandma, as if he were searching for any indication that this might all be an elaborate joke.

"Mia was among those abducted and subjected to experiments. She discovered that I was listed as an emergency contact for one of the DFOG scientists. She managed to escape after enduring eleven years of captivity. It was a harrowing journey for her to find me and share her knowledge of DFOG. But what's most shocking is that the DFOG scientists—one is my son, and the other is his wife. They are at the forefront of these experiments. I thought of you when I learned of this information due to your FBI connections. I think it's important that they be informed of what's going on. Maybe you could reach out to your contact there."

Sheriff Reid rose from his seat, shook his head vigorously, as if trying to clear his thoughts, and raised his hands in a "wait a minute" gesture. "Let me see if I've got this straight. You're claiming there's a secret military base out there creating hybrid soldiers, and Mia is one of them?" He didn't wait for an answer. "I'm sorry, Dr. Porter, but I find that hard to believe."

"I understand how unbelievable this all sounds. I, too, couldn't accept it until I saw it with my own eyes.

"Saw what, exactly?"

"Her transformation." My grandma glanced at Mia. "I think you'll need to show him."

Mia's gaze fixated on the gun holstered at Sheriff Reid's hip before returning to meet his eyes. She tilted her head slightly before she rose from the sofa. "Sheriff," she said calmly, "I need you to disarm your weapon."

He huffed. "Hand over my gun?" His hand instinctively moved to rest on his holster. "You must understand how absurd that sounds, especially after what Dr. Porter just told me."

"I won't harm you, but what about my safety?"

He tightened his grip on his holster as he stared at her. "I'm afraid I can't do that. I'm responsible for everyone's safety, even my own."

"I'm about to transform into something you've never seen before, and I would prefer not to be shot in the process." She kept her composure, even as the tension in the room rose. "I'm not a threat, Sheriff, so I'll ask again if you could disarm."

He maintained an authoritative posture, arms crossed firmly over his chest. "Disarming my weapon is not up for discussion, Mia, but I assure you, I have no intention of shooting you."

I rose from the sofa and moved to Mia's side. "You can trust him. I won't let him shoot you."

My grandma stood as well and added to my sentiments. "He's a man of his word, Mia. Go ahead and show him."

"Okay." The word barely left her lips as her eyes shifted into bright gold and her pupils shrank. The sun's rays caught her razor-sharp fangs and deadly claws, making them appear even creepier in the morning light. She reminded me of a wolf ready to hunt its prey. Hank and Gracie sensed the change and jumped up and stood by her side like guards.

Sheriff Reid slowly stepped back, and his mouth fell open, while his hand hovered over his holster, but as promised, he didn't draw it and aim it at Mia. "Jesus," he uttered, taking another step away from her.

Mia quickly reverted back, like flicking a light switch. Her turquoise eyes gazed at him, her canines receded, and her fingernails replaced her claws, and once again she stood beside me in her human form. Hank and Gracie relaxed, reclaiming their spot by the fireplace. Mia offered a slight smile to Sheriff Reid. "I'm sorry, but you had to see my other side to believe. I escaped from DFOG, but others remain captive, forced to serve as super soldiers under them. Will you help us?"

He blinked several times, his initial shock gradually changing to curiosity. "I've never seen anything like this in my lifetime," he admitted. "But if what you're saying is true, I can't just stand by." He took out his cell phone. "Give me a few minutes." Then, he walked out of the room and into the hallway.

I wrapped my arm around her shoulders, and she leaned against me. "Are you okay?" I asked.

She nodded but remained silent, but her expression seemed troubled.

"We're going to fix this," Grandma stated firmly. "One way or another, I promise you that."

"It's okay, Evelyn. I know that you and Ethan didn't know what was going on, and I'm thankful for your support. It means a lot." She paused, her eyes darting between us. "I think your son and his wife," she looked at me, "your parents, saw merging human and animal DNA as just another step in evolution, not realizing our suffering. Maybe DFOG is the mastermind behind all of this, and we're all victims." Mia sighed deeply. "I remember hearing DFOG guards talk about us as if we were nothing more than tools to accomplish their agendas. All they cared about was power, willing to sacrifice anyone for military gains."

"That's why I think we should call Mom and Dad, Grandma," I reiterated.

Grandma paused, her brow furrowed in thought. "If they're truly unaware, they might be in danger if DFOG discovers we contacted them. Worse, they could feel compelled to act against us to protect themselves."

Sheriff Reid returned to the living room, a hint of shock lingering on his face, pausing my response. "My FBI contact informed me that the Bureau of Supernatural Investigation (BSI) has been tracking DFOG for some time. BSI agents have conducted multiple voluntary interviews at the DFOG headquarters, as well as executed several search warrants, but have had no luck locating the soldiers, mostly because of the tight security around DFOG's operations. Getting verifiable information is tough. The military has denied any knowledge of the super soldiers, which further complicates their investigation. When I told my FBI contact about Mia and her experience, he contacted BSI. They immediately returned his call, expressed a strong interest in speaking with Mia, and quickly arranged to board a plane. They're already en route to Doford Peaks and should arrive in about two hours." He turned to Mia. "I took the liberty of authorizing the interview, based on our conversation here, and I also assumed, Mia, you'd agree."

Mia pressed her lips into a thin line and nodded despite the uncertainty lingering in her gaze. "I'm willing to talk to them. Honestly, I just want this whole thing to be over."

"I think we all want that." He turned to my grandma. "Dr. Porter, I hope you don't mind, but I arranged for them to conduct the interview here, at your house."

"Not at all. My home is a much more comfortable environment for Mia. No one wants to sit in a formal interrogation room."

Mia squeezed my hand. "You'll be there with me, right?"

I held her hand tightly. "Of course."

CHAPTER 8

We gathered around the dining room table. I sat next to Mia, our fingers intertwined and resting on the surface. My grandma occupied one end of the table, while Sheriff Reid sat at the other. BSI agents Ace Gibson and Aurora Cooper sat at the opposite end, facing Mia and me.

Cooper, dressed in a dark suit, appeared to be in her late thirties, standing about 5'7" with an athletic build, like someone who spent a lot of time at the gym. Her intense gray eyes focused on Mia. Her deep brown hair, almost black, pulled back into a ponytail, revealed a small crescent-shaped scar near her left eyebrow. She wore a silver ring, with a pattern of intertwining vines and thorns etched into the metal. It looked like one of those vampire daylight rings from the movies.

Gibson, pushing fifty, stood well over 6 feet tall and had salt-and-pepper hair, with more gray at his temples and in his sideburns. He kept his hair short and neat, like a military cut. A five o'clock shadow lined his jaw, and his brown eyes were unreadable and fixed on Mia. He was also in a dark suit that barely contained his solid frame.

At their request, Mia recounted her story—a tale I had heard three times before—and revealed her wolf side. Gibson and Cooper remained unfazed, their faces expressionless as if it were just another day at the office.

"We have been tracking the DFOG for years," Gibson confirmed. "However, we haven't determined the exact location of the super soldiers. Yes, we're aware of the military base. We just do not know the location where they are holding these soldiers. Without substantial evidence, we haven't been able to press charges.

"Early on in our investigation, our intel led us to a DFOG mission, but it was inaccurate. When we arrived on the scene, it was after the fact, and what we found were several deceased super soldiers. Their bodies were transported to our crime lab for analysis. CSI discovered that a wolf virus had been injected into these soldiers, using advanced CRISPR technology to alter their DNA. Our study also indicated that the DNA mutation seemed to possess regenerative properties. Though, it remains unclear why these soldiers were unable to heal themselves and ultimately died."

A wave of nausea washed over me at the thought that my parents developed a virus to inject into innocent people. How twisted was that? How were these people even my parents? I had nothing in common with them.

"We have conducted multiple infiltrations of their facility, armed with warrants, and searched every floor. However, we have yet to uncover any credible evidence of a research laboratory or medical wing, nor have we managed to expose or reveal these covert activities within their facility." Gibson paused and laid five photographs from a folder in his binder onto the table. Three of the photos were of military men, while the other two were, unfortunately, my parents.

My dad's brown curly hair had that professional slicked-back look that I'd seen in all the family pictures. His brown eyes were focused on something not in the photo, and he was smiling, which was unlike him. He never smiled. My mom's bright red hair fell in waves over her shoulders. Her green eyes had that look of curiosity, like a scientist. Despite not smiling, her expression held a sense of warmth.

Closing my eyes for a few seconds, I pushed aside my awful parents and then centered on the other photos. DFOG was the common thread between the three men. In the first photo, a man in his early fifties had amber eyes, meticulously kept blond hair, and a confident stare. The man in the second photo was in his mid-forties, had green eyes framed by crow's feet, and had chestnut brown hair that exceeded military regulations in length. Finally, the third photo was of the youngest of the three men, maybe around forty. He had brownish-green eyes and short reddish-brown hair kept short.

"Mia, do you recognize any of these individuals?" Gibson asked.

She pointed to the first photo. "That's Colonel Marc Bennett." She tapped the second photo. "That's Major Tony Royce." She gestured to the third photo. "That's my captain, Captain Greg Turner." Lastly, she revealed the unavoidable fact, "These two are Dr. Porter and Dr. Owen."

And I added, "They're my parents."

"Dr. Porter is my son," Grandma said. "But I assume you already knew that."

"Yes, we did make that connection," Gibson confirmed.

Cooper's gaze shifted to Mia. "Our team investigated the terrorist attack on the hospital. We know that the DFOG team you were part of was deployed to rescue the hostages, and we're also aware of the events that followed. That hospital was reduced to ashes," Cooper stated matter-of-factly. "The terrorists detonated explosives, erasing all evidence, including any remains. All cameras, both inside and outside the hospital, as well as in the surrounding area, were destroyed. Consequently, no footage exists of your escape. Your uniform, gear, and tracker were all in the hospital when it was destroyed. Based on that information, DFOG is under the impression that you were one of the deceased. You are, in fact, free, Mia. This is why accepting our request will be even more challenging."

Gibson leaned in, his tone pressing. "Although DFOG believes you are dead, we have an advantage in bringing you back to life and partnering with us. We need you to go undercover for us. You can gather information and help us shut down their operations. With your help, we can free the remaining soldiers."

"I don't know exactly where our barracks are. We were blindfolded when going to and from the barracks for missions," Mia explained. "But I'm sure we were on a lower level. When we left the base, we always took an elevator up, and when we returned, we went down."

The agents exchanged glances, suggesting a silent understanding between them, before nodding, and Cooper began filling us in. "We could simulate a capture-and-trade scenario. We'll equip you with a hidden earpiece for communication with our team. In your wolf form, you'll be convincingly restrained, using special breakaway cuffs, to avoid arousing suspicion as we bring you into the DFOG command center. Claiming we have one of their super soldiers, we'll demand to see Colonel Bennett before creating a distraction, giving you the opportunity to escape. There will be two BSI teams. One will go with you to locate the soldiers, and the other will control the front." Cooper looked at Mia with compassion. "We realize this is a significant request, but you are our best chance at finding the remaining soldiers."

My grandma anxiously drummed her fingers on the table, her eyes narrowed as she took in every word. Sheriff Reid leaned back in his chair, arms crossed, with that same skeptical expression on his face. From my vantage point, I could see the gears turning in Mia's head. She squeezed my hand and took a deep breath, the kind of breath a person makes when they are confronting something terrifying. I feared that she was contemplating reentering the world she had fought so hard to escape from.

"And what about my protection? This is a military black site filled with highly trained soldiers. I can't take them all on."

Gibson plastered a stern expression on his face as he looked directly at Mia. "I'm not going to lie. It's risky. But we have a solid plan and well-trained agents, and they will be with you, and your safety is our top priority. If anything goes wrong, we'll get you out. We're going in together, and we're coming out together."

My hand trembled as I held hers, and I whispered, "He's right. This is too dangerous. You've been through so much already, and I can't bear the thought of losing you. Think about the life you have now. You're happy. Is this mission worth risking what you have?" I silently urged her to choose safety over sacrifice.

She looked at me, tears shimmering in her eyes. "I have to do this, Ethan. It's for the others who are still trapped. I can't let their suffering go on."

I raised my chin, trying to project confidence. "Then I'm going with you."

A few tears slipped down her cheeks as she pressed my hand to her face.

My grandma, on the other hand, was not pleased with my decision. Raising her voice, she insisted, "Absolutely not. Those agents are trained in what they do. They know how to stay safe and handle any situations that might arise." She reached across the table, taking my free hand in both of hers. "You're smart and strong, but this task isn't something you can just tag along for. Plus, there's your asthma. What if something happened to you out there?" Her voice softened as she continued, "Sometimes being brave means understanding your limits, Ethan. Let the SBI do their job. I need you here. Safe with me, okay?"

Cooper interjected. "Your grandmother is right. I understand your desire to help, and I respect that. However, a covert mission is unpredictable. We spend years training for this—learning how to blend in seamlessly and how to detect the slightest sign of trouble." Her tone shifted to a more serious note. "And you aren't trained for this. You don't know our protocols. If something goes wrong, there isn't a civilian backup plan. You would be putting your life, Mia's life, and ours at risk. We can't afford to make any mistakes out there. Allow us to do our job. That's how you can truly help."

When they said no, I was devastated, but my gaze remained fixed on Mia. Her eyes said something much more powerful than words could. As she gripped my hand, it seemed she was silently telling me to ignore them and stand with her. Her slight nod and the way she edged closer to me validated my suspicions despite the disapproval that surrounded us.

"Can I offer a suggestion?" I asked the agents.

Gibson nodded. "Go ahead."

I turned to my grandma first, my heart aching as I swallowed hard, knowing she wouldn't be pleased, but I had to speak up. "Grandma, I love and respect you, but I'm an adult. I would appreciate your support, but I don't need your permission." I then faced the agents and outlined my plan. "I think a hostage-and-demand scenario would be more effective than a capture-and-trade scenario. Mia could hold me hostage and force her way into the DFOG building with her claws at my neck. She would either demand to see the colonel and my parents or threaten to slash my throat. I bet that would get their attention, and they'd come running. Mia could signal you once my parents and the colonel neared us, and then you could rush in. Mia could break away and search for the soldiers with the team you mentioned, and the other team could maintain the front."

The agents exchanged glances, their expressions shifting from skepticism to intrigue. "It's risky," Gibson admitted. "But it might just work. We would need to ensure that every move is calculated and that we have a backup plan in case things go south."

"Ethan, no," Grandma objected, her voice quivering. She turned her attention to Gibson and Cooper, raising her hands in protest. "Just moments ago, he was untrained, oblivious to your protocols, and ready to jeopardize everyone's lives. Now, he is a member of the team. No!"

Mia looked at me as if we were the only two people in the room. Her eyes sparkled with warmth that I loved, and she tightened her grip on my hand, pressing it against her heart. That gesture meant everything to me. In that moment, the opinions of the agents and my grandma faded away; she needed my help.

"Dr. Porter, I agree with you," Cooper stated. "Ethan's proposal carries significant risk, as Gibson has pointed out." She raised her hand to pause my grandma's impending response. "However, the simulation is highly credible, which means we could safely extract Ethan from the building."

"I don't like it," Grandma grumbled.

"Grandma, I have to do this. I want to do this. You said we needed to fix this. My parents did this. Your son did this. We owe it to Mia."

Tears moistened my grandma's eyes, and her chin quivered. She stared at me for several moments before giving a slight nod. I stood up and hugged her tightly. Her arms enveloped me in a fierce embrace, and I felt as though she'd never let go. When she finally pulled away, her gaze turned to the agents. "Make sure no harm comes to my grandson."

***

Two hours later, we were on a flight to Dencester, a major city in Baymont, which was apparently the headquarters of both DFOG and BSI, and a team of agents would be waiting for us at the airport.

My seat and Mia's were directly behind Gibson's and Cooper's. Mia still clung to my hand, and I hadn't released hers. Although she had experience with missions, I sensed she was worried about being captured by DFOG, failing to rescue the soldiers, or something happening to me. On the other hand, my stomach twisted into knots. My grandma and the agents were right. I had no clue what I was getting into and had no business being involved with this situation. All I could focus on was staying by Mia's side, but doubts began to creep in. Maybe my presence was more of a burden than a benefit, but the warmth of Mia's hand in mine grounded me and eased my anxiety somewhat.

"Are you scared?" I whispered in her ear.

"A little. They're putting so much trust in me. What if I don't deliver?" she whispered back.

"Don't think like that. Remember how you managed the situation with Wally and Randy? You took care of me, too. You're brave and strong. You've got this."

She rested her head on my shoulder but didn't say anything. Wrapping my arm around her

shoulders, I pulled her closer, wanting her to feel my belief in her.

I needed to be strong for both of us and for my grandma back home. She put a ton of inhalers in my bag, and I had to laugh. It was clear that she was worried about me and about how we wouldn't be able to communicate during the mission. Before we got on the plane, I texted her.

We're boarding, Grandma.

I love you, Ethan, and be careful.

I will, and I love you, too.

Gibson told me I could text her again when we landed, but after that, I had to stop all communication. Grandma would have her hands full with taking care of Hank and Gracie and her patients at the clinic. Hopefully that would keep her mind occupied and help prevent her from worrying. I was going to miss her and my wolves like crazy. I had never been away from either of them before, but I had Mia, and we held each other for the rest of the flight without saying a word.

Other conversations floated around us, and every so often, I heard the rattle of a beverage cart. To everyone on the plane, we probably looked like your typical young couple traveling together to some fun place. However, she and I were well aware that was not the case, and as the minutes ticked by, we drew closer to our destination. All too quickly the announcement came over the microphone instructing us to fasten our seat belts. I jumped in my seat, and Mia tightened her grip on my hand as the plane began its descent. Anxiety and tension bubbled up within me as I knew once we landed our lives would drastically change, and I wasn't truly ready for that, but it was too late to turn back now.

***

We gathered our overnight bags and followed the agents off the plane. Hurrying passengers brushed past us, their suitcases rolling behind them. Mia and I held hands as we navigated through the crowd, trailing the agents. They led us to a large gray van that looked just like any other van, except for its tinted windows. Aside from that, it blended seamlessly with the other parked cars and taxis in the pickup zone. Gibson motioned for us to enter through the side door, which he had pulled open for us. After stepping inside the van, we dropped our bags on the floor.

Heavy blackout curtains covered the windows inside the van, making me feel slightly claustrophobic and uneasy. The cramped interior contained a cluster of flat-screen monitors mounted on one wall. Wires snaked across the floor, linking microphones, cameras, and recording equipment. The agents, one woman and four men, occupied four swivel chairs and one in the driver's seat with headphones draped around their necks.

The agent behind the wheel started the engine and pulled out of the parking area. Within minutes, we were on the road traveling toward DFOG. A focused silence enveloped the van, broken only by the hum of the engine and the sound of tires on the road. The agents reviewed their equipment, checked surveillance feeds, adjusted microphones, and checked their weapons.

Gibson and Cooper guided Mia and me to a bench positioned against the wall.

"Please take a seat," Gibson instructed. "We'll get you both set up."

Mia tucked her long hair behind her ears while Cooper fitted a discreet earpiece on her, and Gibson attached a matching earpiece on me.

"Test channel," Cooper said into a mic, checking their connections.

"I heard it," Mia confirmed.

My response was a thumbs up.

Gibson nodded, looking satisfied, and then took two slim phones off the counter and handed one to each of us. "These phones are preset. If you need anything, use channel two. Our team in the van will monitor the feed the entire time, and the other team will eventually join you two in DFOG."

"The code word for the breach is 'help,'" Cooper informed us. "Once we hear that word, we'll come in, guns drawn. Mia, you'll break away with Gibson and his team to find the soldiers while my team secures the lobby. Ethan, an agent will escort you back to the van."

Mia slipped her phone into her pocket, a hint of nervousness flickering in her eyes. I felt nervous too, but I gave her a quick, reassuring smile—like, we can do this!

The van wound its way through a series of turns, causing us to shift subtly from side to side on the bench. Occasionally, it slowed down, like maybe navigating traffic or stopping at a light. Those were just guesses since the view outside remained obscured by the blackout curtains. Still, judging by the agents' expressions, it seemed we were getting closer to DFOG.

"Mia, Ethan, I wanted to go over the plan one more time in detail," Gibson reiterated, pausing to pull up a photo on his cell phone. A tannish building resembling a hospital or an institute came into view. "DFOG sits in the heart of the city, and the building blends in seamlessly—government signage, a standard lobby, and nothing to indicate it's anything other than a government building. Based on Mia's statement, we believe the soldiers are being held in a black site located in the basement."

"This plan relies heavily on your actions, Mia," Cooper emphasized. "You'll have already shifted—and you'll be posing a threat to Ethan. That alone could attract attention, both on the sidewalk and as you enter the building."

"That's why I'm wearing a hoodie," Mia interrupted. "I'll pull the hood over my face to conceal my wolf side until we get inside the building."

Gibson nodded in agreement. "Smart. Proceed directly to the security desk and execute the simulation as planned. Insist on seeing Bennett, Porter, and Owen. Make it clear that you will not leave until you have seen them."

Cooper added, "Security might call for backup or claim that the colonel or the doctors aren't available. If you notice any signs of a trap, don't hesitate to use the code word. We'll enter the building right away."

"If the mission goes as planned," Gibson said, raising his voice to make his point. "Use the code the instant you make eye contact with our targets. We'll be in position and ready to move on your signal."

The van came to a stop, and the monitors flickered to life. The live feed displayed the rear of a large, vacant warehouse.

"We're parked a safe distance from DFOG. The address of the building is 13300 Mill Boulevard. Remember, trust your instincts. Are you ready to proceed?"

"I'm ready," Mia replied.

Gibson reached for the door.

"Wait," I called out. I turned to Mia, cupped her face in my hands, and pressed my lips against hers. I kissed her softly, tenderly, and passionately, as if it were the last time I would ever kiss her.

Mia leaned into my kiss, her eyes fluttering shut. When we separated, her fingers gently brushed against my cheek.

"Ah, young love," Gibson grumbled. "Just wait a few years, kids. Things will change."

Cooper dismissed Gibson's comment with a wave of her hand. "Don't pay attention to him. Relationships aren't his strong suit."

"We have a saying at the start of every mission." Gibson paused to slide the van door open. "Don't get dead."

With a hint of sarcasm, I thought, "Wow, that was reassuring. Something I could have done without." Judging by the look on Mia's face, she felt the same way.

We jumped out of the van and stood side by side, watching the door close in front of us. Taking the back streets, we stayed out of sight as long as possible, but eventually, we were forced to move out in the open to enter the building. Mia pulled her hood over her head and sprang into action. Shifting into her wolf form, she clamped her claws around my neck, securing me in a headlock. I hesitated and started to doubt the sanity of our plan, but the people walking nearby didn't seem to notice or care. Perhaps they simply wanted to avoid getting involved in what was going on.

Mia leaned closer, her warm breath against my ear. "Just relax. This is all part of the plan."

I steadied my breathing, trying to prevent an asthma attack. Even though I was aware of our scheme, I reminded myself that maintaining this ruse was vital to achieving our goal. Pushing aside the unsettling sensation of her claws, I concentrated on the tall, mundane tan building that dominated the block. The rows of windows glimmered in the sunlight, while metal frames bordered the double glass doors. As we passed through them, I glanced up to read the sign, "Defense Forces of Genesis."

The lobby had a massive marble desk with a security guard stationed in front of it. Behind the desk sat four individuals clad in military attire, their eyes narrowing as they observed Mia and me. When she threw back her hood, her glowing eyes, fangs, and the claws embedded in my neck were fully exposed, causing the four individuals to spring out of their seats. The guard aimed his gun at us. Using me as a shield, Mia shouted, "Call Colonel Bennett, Dr. Porter, and Dr. Owen down to the lobby, or I will slash his neck! The doctors will care about his pretty neck, considering he's their son."

One of the individuals behind the desk quickly grabbed the phone and relayed Mia's demands. Moments later, the elevator hummed to life, and the doors slid open. My parents rushed out first, closely followed by Colonel Bennett. Colonel Bennett's eyes grew wide as they landed on Mia. My parents had similar expressions. "Mia, thank God you're alive," Colonel Bennett uttered.

Whether he was truly relieved or just acting, I couldn't tell.

From the corner of my eye, I caught Mia squinting at something inside the elevator. When the doors closed, she swiftly turned her gaze toward the colonel and my parents. "Save it, Colonel. I know you could care less about my well-being." She sharpened her tone. "Take me to the soldiers, or he dies!"

Wait a minute. That wasn't the plan. She was supposed to say the code word as soon as she made eye contact? "Don't go rogue on me, Mia," I thought to myself.

"Ethan!" my mother cried. "What on earth are you doing here, and with her?"

"Stay back!" Mia warned.

My dad raised his hands in a gesture of surrender. "Let's discuss this, Mia."

"Just like you talked to us before injecting us with a virus! We never got a choice, and neither do you. Take me to the soldiers!"

I wanted to shout, "What the hell are you doing? Stick to the plan! Say the code word!" But all I could do was stare at my horrible parents, feeling nausea rise in my throat.

Colonel Bennett took a step forward, and Mia's claws dug into my skin, sending a sharp, smarting pain through my neck. Warm liquid began to drip down my skin. "That's my blood! I'm bleeding!" I screamed in my head. Doubt came over me. Was I in danger? Had she deceived me? Was this all just about her and the soldiers?

"Mia, I'll escort you to the soldiers myself," the colonel said, though his words sounded hollow. "Just let him go, or I'll have to call for backup."

She trembled, then stiffened, her silence stretching for several tense seconds as she held onto me. Suddenly, she screamed, "Nobody can help you now, Colonel! Your time just ran out."

Armed agents wearing bulletproof vests and jackets emblazoned with SBI logos rushed through the glass doors. Their boots pounded against the floor as they secured control of the lobby. Cooper and Gibson leveled their guns, shouting, "Hands up and get on the floor!"

Mia reverted back into her human form and released her grip on me. I stumbled forward, my hand instinctively moving to my neck to wipe away the blood.

The lobby erupted into chaos, with SBI agents shouting commands with the physical threat of weapons drawn and ready. Despite knowing how things were going to unfold, the harsh reality of the plan hit me hard. Gibson rushed over to Mia and me, handing us vests. "Put these on, and then we'll proceed, checking floor by floor. Ethan, go with Agent Marsh. He'll take you to the van."

"No," I protested. "I'm not leaving Mia."

"Stick to the plan," Gibson ordered.

"Change of plans," I insisted.

"He stays, or I don't follow through with this mission," Mia retorted with an ultimatum.

"Shit," Gibson grumbled, and then pointed at Mia. "If anything happens, it's on you, Mia. Let's move out."

Mia slipped on the vest and bobbed her head toward the colonel. "We need the colonel or one of his parents to come with us, and I need a gun."

"No and no. I've already broken protocol by letting Ethan tag along. Going forward, my mission. My orders." Gibson scowled. "Move."

Mia stood her ground. "I'm military trained, fully capable of handling a weapon, and you can't predict what might happen inside this building. Plus, like you said, if anything happens, it's on me, so I need a gun. Also, you're wrong. We have to take one of them with us. I saw the reflection of a retinal scanner on the mirrored wall of the elevator. That must be how they're accessing the basement, so we bring one of them, or I cut out an eyeball. Your choice."

Cooper kept her gaze fixed on her targets lying on the floor in the lobby as she commanded, "Take the mother and give Mia a gun, Gibson."

Gibson turned to one of the agents and instructed, "Check the elevator for a retinal scanner."

The agent quickly approached the elevator a few feet away from us and pressed the call button. The doors slid open, and the agent glanced inside before jogging back to report to Gibson. "Affirmative. A retinal scanner is present."

"Thanks for the vote of confidence," Mia retorted sarcastically. "As if I would lie about it. We need to trust each other and work together, or this mission is going to fail."

I frowned as I stared at Mia, wondering, "Who is this girl?" This Mia was sarcastic, bold, and a bit reckless. I wasn't sure I liked this side of her. I missed the gentle, thoughtful Mia I cared about, the one who always listened and responded with kindness. It felt as though I was looking at a stranger.

Mia caught me staring, and it seemed she sensed my thoughts. Her face softened, and her eyes showed that she was sorry. "I don't mean to come off as harsh, but my adrenaline is pumping. I can't let myself become a victim again."

I was on the verge of responding when Gibson huffed and muttered something under his breath before passing Mia a gun. He then turned to the same agent and barked, "Get the mother."

My mom gasped, and my dad jumped to his feet, shouting, "Take me. Let me go instead."

Cooper yelled, "On the floor, Porter! Now!"

My dad lowered himself back down, a groan escaping his lips. He lay motionless as the agent grasped my mom's arm, lifted her off the floor, and marched her over to where Gibson was standing. My mom didn't look at me or anyone for that matter. Her eyes were focused on the floor.

Gibson and Cooper exchanged nods, again signaling some sort of agreement. Six agents broke away and joined Gibson, while eight agents remained with Cooper.

"With me," Gibson ordered and headed toward the elevator.

My mom, Mia, and I followed Gibson's team to the elevator. It swiftly opened, and the ten of us crowded inside. Gibson glanced at my mom and gestured toward the retinal scanner. She stood still, refusing to move, and the agent beside her pushed her forward until she was an inch away from the scanner. My mom tucked her chin down, avoiding eye contact. It took two agents to lift her head and pry her eyelid open with their fingers and hold it steady against the scanner.

As my mom stood there, forced to remain still, the retinal scanner whirred to life. A thin, glowing blue line scanned across her pupil, veri-fying identity. The display screen morphed from blue to green, granting access, and the elevator jolted downward. A digital voice verbalized, "Good afternoon, Dr. Owen. Proceeding to the basement."

The elevator descended, plunging us deeper into the facility. No one spoke as the elevator glided past the floors; the only sound was the whirring of gears.

Gibson broke the silence, asking, "What's the layout of the basement?"

Everyone turned to my mom, but she remained silent.

It was Mia who spoke up. "I believe it's divided into three wings: medical, research, and our quarters, but since we were blindfolded, I can't be certain."

Gibson gestured toward my mom. "You're our guide, whether you like it or not. But first, we need to exit this elevator safely. I'm certain a DFOG team was dispatched and will be waiting for us. Everyone, keep clear of the doors and aim at the opening, prepared to fire. Do you copy?"

Everyone but my mom and me nodded in agreement. We just stood there, like a couple of senseless zombies without a clue how to dodge incoming bullets.

"Passing Sublevel," the digital voice announced. The monitor flashed red, displaying the word "Basement," as the elevator gradually came to a halt. The agents quickly assumed defensive positions, raising their guns as the doors began to part.

Just outside the elevator, armed guards rushed into view, leaving me with no time to react as bullets ricocheted off the elevator's surface. I pressed myself against the wall, flattening my body as much as possible.

Gibson shouted above the chaos, "Aim for fatal shots!"

Straightaway, one of Gibson's agents positioned herself at the edge of the door and fired a precise shot, striking the nearest guard squarely in the chest and sending him slumping to the ground. A second agent, crouched low, unleashed a rapid burst of bullets—pop, pop, pop. Two of the bullets struck another guard, hitting him once in the neck and once in the gut. The man crumpled to the ground, his weapon skidding across the polished floor.

The remaining three DFOG guards charged the elevator, but Gibson's agent tossed some kind of a grenade into the corridor. An extremely loud boom and blinding flash filled the space, disorienting the guards. Seizing the opportunity, Gibson and his team took aim and fired several rounds. Two more guards fell—one sagged against the far wall, while the other dropped in mid-sprint.

The last guard fired recklessly into the elevator, bullets striking the metal walls just inches from our heads. Gibson remained unfazed. He took aim and, with one decisive shot, eliminated the guard. Utter silence fell over the corridor. Cautiously, we inched out of the elevator and into the hallway, where five motionless bodies lay sprawled across the polished tile.

Gibson lowered his weapon and called out, "Clear."

My legs wobbled as I stood in the center of the corridor, staring at the lifeless bodies; the echoes of gunfire still rang in my ears. A metallic taste coated the back of my throat, and my nose burned. Was the feeling real or psychological? Panic hit, and I ran my hands over my chest, checking for wounds. Thank God, no bullets had struck me or anyone else on Gibson's team. It felt like a miracle or something.

An arm came around me. I jumped and spun around, relieved to find Mia by my side. She pulled me close and asked, "Are you okay?"

I trembled uncontrollably as I clung to her. We stood in the middle of dead guards, their blood pooling on the floor. The dark red was repulsively noticeable under the harsh glare of fluorescent lights. "No, I'm not okay. None of this is okay."

Before Mia could respond, Gibson ordered, "Grab their rifles and gear. We can use the extra ammo." His gaze scanned the area, taking in the surroundings. "Keller, Hayes, Pierce, and Harper, you're with me. Briggs and Locke, go with Mia and Ethan. Take the mother with you. Make sure she cooperates and leads you to the soldiers."

With all the insane stuff happening around us, I hadn't really paid attention to any of the agents. They kind of blurred together—just a bunch of people with guns, running everywhere. But when Gibson broke up the team, Briggs and Locke stood in front of us, making them impossible to ignore. They seemed younger than Gibson, maybe in their thirties, with that typical military look—buzz cuts, built like linebackers, the whole deal. Where Briggs seemed chill, Locke was the guy who'd pick a fight just to see what would happen.

Briggs was the taller one, probably six-three or six-four, with broad shoulders that made his tactical vest look a size too small. His hair was a sandy blonde, cut short but messy around the edges, and he had these calm, navy blue eyes that didn't judge. A permanent dimple was on his left cheek, and he had this chill way of standing that made him look like nothing could faze him.

Locke was a few inches shorter, with dark hair cropped close to his head. There was a thin scar running from his temple down to his eyebrow, making him look tough, like he'd been through some serious stuff. His arms were covered in tattoos—some military, some not—snaking down to his wrists. His eyes were quick and restless, always scanning the area around him, and he had this crooked smirk that made it clear he was probably trouble, or at least wanted you to think so.

My mom sighed in frustration, turning my focus on her. "Stop calling me 'the mother.' I have a name. It's Dr. Owen."

I rolled my eyes at the irony and shot back, "Yeah, I agree. 'Mother' is definitely the wrong label. She certainly isn't winning any mother of the year awards after abandoning me when I was five."

My mom squeezed her eyes shut and groaned. "Ethan, don't start with me."

I thrust my hand in her direction. "You forfeited the right to tell me what to do a long time ago."

Gibson raised his hands in a calming gesture. "All right, everyone. Let's settle down. This isn't the time or place to dredge up family disputes. Mia, when you reach the soldiers, assure them we're on their side. We could use their help getting back to the lobby safely."

"Will do."

There was so much more I could say, but I clamped my mouth shut. My mom didn't care what I thought. She never listened to me, not ever. I'd be wasting my breath. I needed to think clearly, and I couldn't do that hanging onto the past. I shook off my frustrations and headed after Briggs and the others.

They led the way into the corridor. Briggs held my mom's arm, while Mia followed closely behind, and I brought up the rear. We reached a corner, and I glanced over my shoulder, taking one last look at Gibson's team. They were positioned around the elevator, weapons raised, and vanished from my sight as we rounded the corner. Ahead of me stretched a long, narrow hallway, empty and with no doors.

Briggs pointed down the corridor. "Is this the way?"

My mom confirmed with only a nod.

An uneasy feeling settled in as I took in the surroundings. Was my mom really leading us to where Briggs and Locke wanted her to take us? I had my doubts. It seemed like we kept repeating the same steps: walk a few feet, come to a corner, turn, and then do it again, like a continuous loop or maze. I couldn't tell where we were anymore. It felt as if we were just walking in circles.

"Okay, Dr. Owen," Briggs stopped and faced my mom. "We've traveled a good twenty minutes, and all I see is an endless hallway. You'd better not be taking us on a wild goose chase. Where are the soldiers?"

She glared at him and didn't say anything.

He turned to Mia. "Any of this familiar?"

Mia shook her head. "No, nothing, but I do remember that we had to walk for quite a while before reaching the elevator."

Locke exhaled sharply. "Listen, Doc, we don't have time to waste. Your sole purpose here is to guide us to their location, so let's get on with it."

"I never agreed to help you. I'm here because I didn't have a choice."

Mia whipped her head around to face my mom. "You hypocrite. That's exactly what you did to me and to the others. I thought you and Dr. Porter saw the project as a step in evolution, not to inflict pain. I was wrong. We didn't have a choice to become these things that you created." Mia walked up to my mom and bluntly retorted, "You disgust me."

Briggs stepped between Mia and my mom. "I understand you have your reasons, but you need to calm down, Mia. The reality is that we need her help."

Mia huffed in frustration and turned her back on them.

"We did this for our son," my mom shot back.

I pointed a rigid finger in my mom's face and yelled, "Don't friggin put this on me. I'm 19 years old. You don't even know who I am. You and Dad did it for fame, for notoriety, and for whatever agreement you made with the military. This has nothing to do with me. You're monsters, not doctors or scientists."

Like she didn't even hear a word I said, she responded, "It was all for you. We needed financial backing and laboratory equipment. So, yes, we collaborated with the military. We presented our proposal, and they accepted. We had to conduct tests, and the military wanted soldiers, but we developed and engineered the virus specifically for you, Ethan, and others with asthma. We had no choice but to test the virus on humans to perfect it and ensure its safety. The virus is your cure, Ethan. Your father and I plan to administer it to you."

I blinked slowly, my body tensing with anger and lips spread into a thin line. I couldn't believe what had just come out of my mom's mouth. Injecting me with a wolf virus? Was she out of her mind?

Mia stepped in front of me, shielding me with her body as she aimed her gun at my mom. "You would do this to your own son? Well, I won't allow you to mutate him with that virus. Who would want to become a hybrid creature? Can't you see the consequences of what you're doing?"

My mom smirked at Mia as she replied, "You know better than anyone that the wolf part of you can always stay hidden. You only show it to intimidate or threaten your rivals. Remember, it was Colonel Bennett's team that trained you to use this tactic, not me or Dr. Porter."

Mia closed the gap between them, her voice low and almost growling as she challenged, "How could you possibly know? The virus isn't in you."

My mom stood tall, asserting, "I believe you take pleasure in the power it grants you."

Mia shoved her gun in my mom's face, and Briggs and Locke intervened, separating them. "Calm down, Mia," Briggs ordered. "This is exactly why Gibson didn't want to give you a gun. You're too emotionally involved to think clearly. If you can't control your emotions, I'll take your gun myself. Are we clear?"

Mia nodded, inching backward, but still glaring at my mom.

My mom whimpered and dropped to her knees, wrapping her arms around her ankles. Her right hand slipped beneath her pant leg, grasping something concealed there. In one swift motion, she shot up to her feet and aimed a gun at Mia.

As Mia stared at the barrel of my mom's gun, I gasped for air and immediately pleaded with myself. *I can't have an asthma attack. Not now!* I quickly reached into my pocket for my inhaler and took a dose of medicine. No one saw me. Everyone's focus was on Mia and my mom.

Mia swiftly raised her gun, which only escalated the situation. They stood a few feet apart, both with their weapons drawn and aimed at one another. My mom's hands trembled as she fought to steady her gun, while Mia's grip on her weapon remained firm. Briggs and Locke flew into combat mode, raising their weapons and aiming at my mom.

"Drop your weapon, Dr. Owen! Now!" Briggs ordered, his voice sharp.

Locke's gaze focused on my mom. "Now's the time, Doc. Put down your weapon."

I shook off the episode, and with my heart pounding inside my chest, I yelled, "Don't shoot! Don't shoot, please!"

Chaos erupted as a struggle broke out between the four of them. In the confusion, I couldn't see who among the tangled bodies had the upper hand. A single shot rang out, thundering in my ears. Mia staggered back, her gun clattering to the floor as blood began to spread just below her collarbone, soaking through the edge of her vest.

Briggs and Locke pounced on Mom, wrestling her to the floor and yanking the gun from her grasp. Locke shoved my mom's hands behind her back and secured them with zip ties.

"No!" I shouted, racing to Mia's side as she crumpled to the ground. Mia gasped, her face growing pale and eyes unfocused. I ripped off my jacket and pressed it hard against her wound. My hands shook as I tried to stop the bleeding. "Hold on, Mia," I pleaded.

Approaching footsteps caught our attention. Briggs and Locke took up a defensive stance, guns raised and aimed at the sound. Two individuals—one woman and one man—dressed in white coats, rushed toward us and skidded to a halt, their eyes widening as they darted back and forth between us. The broad-shouldered man with ashy blonde hair in a crew cut, along with an unkempt, scruffy beard covering the lower part of his face, seemed confused. His hazel eyes bulged as they landed on my mom, and he shouted, "Dr. Owen, what is happening?"

The woman's curly brown hair piled on top of her head suggested that her appearance wasn't a top priority. The glasses balanced on the tip of her nose threatened to fall off as she gasped, "Oh, my God, it's Mia." Unfazed by the guns, she rushed to Mia and me. Her amber-colored eyes locked on mine as she ordered, "Let me check the wound."

I lifted my jacket off Mia and scooted back. Briggs and Locke maintained their protective stances, guns still aimed. Briggs shouted, "Who are you people?"

The man raised his hands in surrender and said, "I'm Dr. Matrey." He gestured toward the woman who was assessing Mia. "That's Dr. Blanchett. We're part of Dr. Flower's team. Why are you holding Dr. Owen? Can you tell us who you are and what you're doing here?"

Briggs pointed at himself. "I'm BSI Agent Briggs." He nodded at Locke. "And this is BSI Agent Locke. That's Ethan next to Mia, the son of Dr. Porter and Dr. Owen. We detained Dr. Owen because she shot Mia."

Dr. Blanchett jerked her head back in surprise. "Dr. Owen, why would you shoot Mia?"

"It was an accident," Mom blurted out.

Briggs grunted. "If your gun hadn't been raised and aimed at Mia, this wouldn't have happened."

Dr. Blanchett seemed disinterested in the specifics and returned her attention to Mia, but her gaze remained fixed on Briggs. "There's an entrance and exit wound. The bullet went straight through."

Briggs scanned the floor and the wall near Mia. "Locke, retrieve Mia's gun and locate the bullet. We need to bag it."

Locke secured Mia's gun and began searching the floor and the wall nearby. His gaze narrowed on a specific spot on the wall. "Found it," he announced. He retrieved a small pocketknife out of his pocket and carefully dug the bullet out of the wall, then placed it into a bag.

Briggs returned his attention to Dr. Matrey. "We're here to locate the soldiers and extract them safely," he explained, "but right now, Mia needs medical attention."

"She's lost a significant amount of blood," Dr. Blanchett observed. "If we can stabilize her, her regenerative abilities should activate and heal the wound."

"Agent Briggs, Mia needs a trauma kit," Dr. Matrey said, his sharp tone emphasizing the severity of the situation. "The medical wing is just down the hall and around the corner. We need to act quickly—"

Briggs cut him off. "We'll go together. No sudden moves. Locke, cover Owen." Briggs gestured with his gun for Dr. Matrey. "Lead the way."

Mia reached for my hand, and I gripped hers tightly. Her voice was barely a whisper as she said, "Don't leave me."

"Not a chance," I reassured her.

We hurried down the hall, with Mia in my arms and Dr. Blanchett in front of me. Locke held on to my mom, and Briggs walked a few steps behind Dr. Matrey as we all followed him to the medical wing.

In less than five minutes, he stopped at one of the many doors and flung it open. Harsh fluorescent lights illuminated an array of monitors, X-ray machines, ventilators, a crash cart, IV bags, instrument trays, and cabinets lining the walls, likely stocked with medical supplies. In the center of the room stood a surgical gurney, and positioned to its right were two exam tables.

"Ethan, place Mia on the table," Dr. Matrey said, pointing in its direction.

Dr. Blanchett wheeled the X-ray machine over to the table and positioned it over Mia's chest. She took a few images before pushing the machine to the side and then listened to Mia's lungs. "Everything sounds normal," she confirmed, turning her focus to the blood exiting her wound.

Examining the X-rays, Dr. Matrey nodded in agreement. "There are no visible bone fractures or bullet fragments, though a surgical exploration will tell us if the X-ray missed anything. There could be possible debris or tissue damage." He started preparing the surgical table. Over his shoulder, he explained, "Gunshot wounds carry debris, which can easily contaminate the injury. Mia, we need to flush and clean both the entrance and exit wounds, then pack them with sterile gauze."

"No anesthesia," Mia insisted. "Do what you have to do, but I'm staying awake." She looked up at me, her expression intense. "Promise, Ethan, that they don't put me under."

I shook my head. "Mia, you can't stay awake for this. It will be too painful."

Dr. Blanchett echoed my words. "He's right, Mia. You won't be able to tolerate the pain, and you won't be able to lie still. The anesthesia is for your safety and to make sure everything goes as smoothly."

Mia clutched my hand, her eyes pleading. "Ethan, please don't let them do this. I need to stay awake!"

I leaned closer to her, gently stroking her hair. "Mia, why is it so important for you to be awake?"

Tears flooded her eyes as she said, "If they put me out, I lose all control, and they take it from me. Please, Ethan!"

I suddenly understood. She had been injected with the virus for years during her imprisonment at DFOG. Now, she found herself back in a vulnerable situation where control was beyond her grasp. She was scared and didn't trust them. My mind raced, trying to recall a past emergency at my grandma's clinic where anesthesia wasn't an option. The scenario gradually surfaced in my mind. A young boy had fallen through a glass window, leaving deep cuts all over his body. I remembered something about him having a reaction to the anesthesia. My grandma used lidocaine instead. Maybe that could work for Mia. I shifted my gaze to the doctors. "What about using lidocaine?"

They exchanged glances, and after a long moment, Dr. Matrey replied, "Yes, that could work."

"Then go with that."

Mia squeezed my hand. "Thank you."

I leaned down and pressed a kiss to her forehead.

Briggs' cell phone rang, breaking the tension in the room. He moved away from the table and pressed the phone to his ear. "Gibson. What's up?" Briggs sighed. "Copy that. We ran into a problem as well. Dr. Owen shot Mia. The bullet went straight through. We're in medical, where she's being treated." Briggs nodded. "Will do." He ended the call and turned to Locke. "Bennett and his DFOG guards tried to overpower Cooper and her team. Cooper's team is holding them off and called backup. Our SWAT team is on its way. Gibson also mentioned his team has seen no activity from the elevator."

Locke clenched his jaw. "Let's hope that's the only surprise we encounter."

Briggs glanced at Mia. "Gibson was relieved to hear that your wound wasn't serious and wants us to stay on mission."

"Mia isn't going anywhere for a while," Dr. Matrey said, injecting lidocaine in and around Mia's wound. "I need to flush the wound, check for any debris or damage, then pack it and apply pressure bandages. I also want to administer IV antibiotics and pain medication."

"Do what you need to do to treat the wound, but no IV," Briggs objected. "There's got to be some oral medication you can give her."

Dr. Matrey protested. "An IV will deliver the medication more quickly into her bloodstream, and—"

Briggs cut him off. "This isn't up for debate. We follow my orders. Dr. Owen failed to follow orders and is now in our custody, so I need one of you to take us to where the soldiers are being held."

"I'll take you," Dr. Blanchett volunteered. "I never liked how DFOG treated them."

"Don't do it, Lucy," Dr. Matrey urged, his face tense.

Locke butted into their conversation, his voice stern. "I don't think any of you understand the seriousness of the situation. We're talking about kidnapping and false imprisonment here. And those experiments—using people as test subjects without their consent? That's not just unethical, it's criminal, and it violates every human rights law on the books. These are all felonies. You could lose everything, your freedom, your jobs, and even your licenses." He stopped for a moment to let his words sink in. "But the worst part of this whole mess is the creation of hybrids for military use. Do you know how illegal that is? There are international treaties against biological weapons and unauthorized genetic engineering. You all knew what was happening here, and none of you came forward. Because of this, you are all considered accessories, and you could all still wind up in jail."

Absorbing Locke's words, they exchanged glances, panic gradually spreading across their faces. It seemed that none of them had considered the possibility of being held accountable.

"We'll take you to them," Dr. Matrey said.

Dr. Blanchett nodded in agreement.

CHAPTER 9

At around 3:00 a.m., we followed the doctors down the same corridor. Briggs was right behind them. Locke trailed Briggs, pulling Dr. Owen along with him. Mia and I were last. After Dr. Matrey treated Mia and applied the pressure bandages, he put Mia's arm in a sling to keep it stable. He'd also given her an antibiotic and a pain injection. In my opinion, she didn't look so good. Her face was pale, and she was hunched over, favoring her shoulder. The healing ability that Dr. Blanchett mentioned kind of worked. It stopped the bleeding, and the wound seemed to be healing, but her pain was definitely evident. She leaned against my side, using me for support. I wrapped my arm around her waist to help keep her steady. For Mia's sake, I hoped the soldiers' location wasn't much farther away.

Briggs and Locke insisted that Mia was essential in getting the soldiers to cooperate and leave with them. Both had the impression that without Mia, the soldiers would resist and wouldn't trust that BSI was there to free them from DFOG. They also worried that the presence of agents could lead to a confrontation, which neither of them wanted. But none of that mattered to me. My only concern was Mia. "How much farther?" I called out.

"We're almost there," Dr. Blanchett said. "About five more minutes."

"Do you want me to carry you?" I whispered to Mia.

She didn't speak, just shook her head no.

After a few more minutes of walking, the corridor simply ended with a blank wall before us. Dr. Matrey pressed his palm against the right side of the concrete, and a hidden compartment in the wall revealed a scanner. He held his face close to the reader, and a thin blue light traced his eye, confirming access. The wall then transformed into a large, thick metal door, which automatically opened, sliding sideways like a pocket door into the wall.

The soldiers' quarters were tucked beneath all the floors of the building, secure and self-contained, and isolated from any glimpse of the outside world. As we entered, warm light spilled across the threshold, illuminating the barracks' front room—the rec room. The space was surprisingly inviting, with smooth, cream-colored walls and soft recessed lighting that banished any hint of gloom. Several soldiers were lounging on a huge gray sectional sofa in the middle of the room, reading or watching the huge 60-foot TV screen on the far wall. The built-in shelves next to it held a wide range of board games, puzzles, and a large library of books. To one side, a pool table awaited players, its green felt surface neatly racked with cues and balls in position.

Off to the right, a glass-paneled section revealed a compact gym. The padded flooring was spotless, and the gym housed several exercise bikes, treadmills, an organized rack of dumbbells, and a pair of sturdy pull-up bars. A few more soldiers were there, engaged in their workouts. A few large potted plants brought a touch of greenery to the corners of the room. Near the gym entrance, a water dispenser stood alongside a bulletin board mounted on the wall overhead, which appeared to display their missions.

The moment we appeared, the soldiers' attention shifted from their screens and workouts to us and then to Mia. One man, with light gray eyes, short jet-black hair, and an extremely muscular build, leaped off a treadmill and rushed over, shouting, "Mia!" As he stopped in front of us, I noticed veins rippling across his forearms.

Within moments, the rest of the soldiers—three women and four men—gathered around Mia. They all looked to be about my age or Mia's. A guy with messy sandy blond hair, a face full of freckles, and wide blue eyes stared at her in disbelief. "I thought you were dead," he blurted out.

The tallest of the group, a man with a scar trailing down his cheek, narrowed his almost-black eyes at Mia and furrowed his thick brows. "I did, too," he said quietly. Beside him stood a girl with the sides of her head shaved and her hair twisted into braids, raising a pierced eyebrow and letting out a huff—was that jealousy?

"Hey Mia, I'm really glad to see you," another guy said, flashing a crooked smile. His copper-red hair, intense green eyes, and compact, muscular build made him look like a comic book superhero.

Finally, the only guy wearing glasses, his long brown hair falling into hazel eyes, stared intently at Mia. Two girls stood on either side of him. One, with shoulder-length black hair pulled back in a ponytail and striking violet eyes, looked like a runner; her long legs and toned arms gave it away. The other had pale skin, chin-length platinum blonde hair, and icy blue, almost translucent eyes that looked almost unreal. The guy standing between them finally broke the silence. "Well, Mia. What gives?"

Mia stayed close to my side, and I kept my arm around her. She remained silent for several seconds and then said, "The hospital mission..." Her voice faded, and she looked to the floor. She took a deep breath and continued, meeting their eyes. "We failed. The terrorists killed my team. To save my life, I stripped out of my gear and changed into a patient's gown. I was released as one of the hostages. Then I did the only thing I knew: I ran to the person I believed could save us."

The girl with the braids sneered at Mia. "That mission was months ago. You know what I think? I think you saved your own ass and fled with no intention of coming back here and saving us."

"Get off your high horse," Locke scoffed. "Any one of you Canine Commandos, given the chance, would have high-tailed it out of here and not looked back. But Mia did come through. Because we're here."

Briggs stepped forward and gestured to himself and Locke. "I'm Agent Briggs, and this is Agent Locke. We're from BSI. DFOG is under our investigation. With Mia's help we were able to infiltrate this facility. There's another team securing the lobby, and SWAT is en route. We'll be bringing all of you out of here."

"Where to?" asked the guy with messy blonde hair.

"To freedom," Locke answered.

The girl with freakish-looking eyes focused on my mom. She tilted her chin toward her and asked, "Why are Dr. Matrey and Dr. Blanchett here, and why are Dr. Owen's hands zip-tied?"

"It's a long story," my mom said, trying to make light of the situation and divert attention away from herself.

Mia whipped her head toward my mom and retorted, "You shot me!"

The soldiers, all of them, wore identical expressions—wide eyes, raised brows, and slack jaws. The girl with the ponytail spoke up. "You shot Mia, Dr. Owen? Why?"

My mom heaved an exaggerated sigh. "It was an accident."

Briggs raised his hand and stopped the conversation. "Let's not rehash this." He turned to the soldiers and rattled off a quick summary. "Dr. Owen held a gun on Mia. There was a struggle, and the gun went off, resulting in Mia being shot." He glanced at Mia. "She's okay. Dr. Matrey and his team came to her aid." Briggs turned his attention back to the soldiers. "Are there any others here with you?"

The guy with gray eyes replied, "Yeah. There are twenty-three soldiers sleeping in their bunks right now."

"Wake them up and bring them back here ready to go," Briggs ordered before turning to Locke. "Locke, you go with him."

"Will do."

Locke followed the guy out of the rec room, and they disappeared down a hallway. An awkward tension filled the room as the soldiers' gazes shifted between Mia and me. I was sure they were wondering who I was. It probably wasn't the best time for me to mention that I was the son of Dr. Porter and Dr. Owen, so I kept quiet. But the girl with the braids had other plans. She stepped forward, her eyes narrowing. "So, are you an agent too or Mia's bodyguard?"

"I'm Ethan. My grandma was the person Mia came to for help." I didn't elaborate. If I said more, I knew it wouldn't end well.

The girl scrunched her face and turned toward Mia. "Why would you go to his grandmother for help?"

"She was listed as an emergency contact for someone in DFOG," Mia said, though the look on her face read, *Why am I even explaining myself to her?* "I didn't know what her connection to DFOG was, but something told me she was my only chance for help."

The soldiers exchanged glances, their expressions reflecting doubt as their gazes shifted to me. In one breath, my mom revealed the truth. "I'm Ethan's mother, and Dr. Porter is his father. Ethan's grandmother is Dr. Porter's mother."

"You went to the mother of the person responsible for all of this?" The girl with braids shouted. "Are you stupid? Why would you think his own mother would betray him?"

Mia clenched her fists and shot back. "Maybe it's you who is stupid. I said I didn't know their connection."

I had to speak up. "None of you know anything about me, my grandma, or my relationship with my parents. Neither I nor my grandma had any idea my parents were involved in this mess." I jutted my hand toward my mom. "This is the first time I've seen her in fourteen years. And Mia did come to my grandma, and my grandma did help. Agent Briggs and Agent Locke are here because of her. So, I'd think twice before making any more accusations when you don't know what you're talking about."

The girl's cheeks turned a shade of pink, and she avoided making eye contact with me. The guy with the scar scooped an arm around her and led her away from me. Briggs patted me on the back before saying, "Our main focus should be on safely and securely extracting all of you from these barracks."

The sound of heavy, synchronized footsteps echoed from the corridor, like a drum of boots against tile. Locke entered the rec room, the guy with gray eyes beside him. Behind them, a line of men and women soldiers marched in, some rubbing their eyes and yawning, and they formed an orderly line in the center of the room. The air shifted as their collective presence filled the space, a silent tension crackling beneath their rigid posture. They snapped to attention, shoulders squared, eyes front—waiting, uncertain.

Briggs waved his hand in a downward motion. "At ease. This isn't a mission. We're here to extract you from the building."

"I gave them the rundown, Briggs," Locke said. "I also mentioned SWAT was on its way."

From among the cluster of soldiers, one stood out: a tall, lean man with shaggy brown hair that stuck damply to his forehead. His eyes, a matching shade of brown, darted anxiously around the room as sweat trickled down his temples. The way he kept swallowing, with his throat bobbing with every nervous gulp, caught my attention. Was he ill? The jittery edge to his movements suggested something closer to fear.

Briggs and Locke noticed the change instantly. Briggs called him out. "Is there a problem, soldier?"

The man's hand rose shakily, revealing a small object clutched in his palm.

"That's a detonator!" someone shouted, the words slicing through the air.

Chaos threatened to erupt. Briggs' and Locke's training took over in an instant. They both drew their weapons, every muscle tense, eyes trained on the man. The rest of the soldiers scattered away from the man.

Briggs' voice was steady, but urgency laced his tone. "Slowly, put it on the floor. Now."

The detonator trembled between the soldier's fingers, a bead of sweat falling from his chin. "I—I haven't activated it," he stammered. "But it's a direct order. I was told that if the DFOG super soldier project was ever exposed—"

Locke cut him off. "Who gave the order? Where's the bomb?"

Panic was etched across the soldier's forehead, his eyes wide and wild. "You don't understand."

Briggs took a careful step closer, gun still trained on the man. "Put down the detonator, and we can talk this through."

The soldier shook his head, sweat now streaming freely. "It's not that simple." His voice trembled, raw fear shining in his eyes. "I am the bomb."

My heart seemed to stop and then jumped into my throat. For a split second, everything around me blurred—faces, voices, and the room. All I could hear was the frantic pounding in my chest, drowning out every other sound. My clammy hand grabbed onto Mia's, and I shielded her as my mind raced with images of what might happen next—flashes of fire, chaos, the unthinkable. The words replayed in my head: I am the bomb. Panic clawed at my insides, but I forced myself to stay calm and hoped that Briggs and Locke could find a way to stop this nightmare before it was too late.

Locke's finger hovered over the trigger, then he lowered it slightly, confusion and horror flickering across his face. "What do you mean you're the bomb?"

The soldier swallowed hard, his whole body trembling. "It's inside me, somewhere. I'm supposed to detonate it if we are ever found out, but I don't want to die!"

Dr. Blanchett inched forward, nervously pushing her glasses upward as she said, "We have to get him to medical and run a full scan. If we can locate the bomb, we might be able to disable it, but we need to act quickly before anything triggers it."

Dr. Matrey joined them, his voice calm but urgent. "We've removed plenty of foreign objects, but never a bomb. If we sedate him, we'll have a better chance at finding it."

"Locke and I have defused many bombs, but never one inside a person," Briggs pointed out. "Though, we may be able to pinpoint its location and determine how to defuse it." Briggs lowered his weapon and asked, "Soldier, what's your name?"

"Todd, Todd Lawson."

"Todd, we're taking you to medical. You're not alone in this, but you have to trust us."

He nodded, his voice trembling. "Just don't let me die. Please!"

"That's the plan," Briggs said calmly. "Locke, keep an eye on things." He faced us and the others and ordered, "The rest of you stay here with Locke."

Briggs stood on one side of Todd and the doctors on the other as they led him away.

What the hell just happened? Had they seriously planted a bomb inside somebody and told them to detonate themselves? Who does that? Monsters, that's who. I turned to face my mom, my eyes narrowed in anger. Could she really be involved in this? Were she and Dad transforming people into hybrids and bombs? I released Mia and faced my mom. "Did you do this? Did you actually implant a bomb inside someone?"

Locke folded his arms and huffed. "I'd like to hear the answer to that, too."

"Of course not," my mom snapped. "Your father and I research ways to cure people, not to harm them. I have no knowledge of any bombs being surgically implanted in anyone." She paused and added, "It did seem odd that those doctors, who are on the surgical team, were unaware of a bomb being implanted in this soldier."

Locke dropped his arms to his sides, a frown appearing on his forehead. "What are you getting at? Are you implying the doctors lied to us?"

"What I'm suggesting is that someone had to insert that bomb." She shrugged. "But it's possible Colonel Bennett has a surgical team I'm not aware of."

Locke approached Mia and handed her a gun. "Watch the room until I get back."

"Locke, wait," Mia cautioned. "I've seen many different doctors here, too many to remember." She shot a glare at my mom. "She might just be trying to bait you into leaving the room."

He tilted his head, his eyes briefly glancing upward before settling on Mia. "Good point. I'll call Briggs to confirm their status." He moved to the other side of the room, his phone pressed to his ear. Moments later, he returned. "The doctors and Briggs are making progress." He fist-bumped Mia's shoulder. "You're okay, Mia. I rather like you."

I pushed my shoulders back and raised my eyebrows at him.

He smirked. "Relax, Porter. I'm not trying to encroach on your territory. I'm just admiring

Mia's solid instincts."

Mia giggled and nudged me, clearly enjoying my hint of jealousy.

Locke turned away from me and Mia and faced the remaining soldiers. "Is there an armory within your barracks? When we move out, everyone needs to be locked and loaded."

"We have an armory, but we can't access it," one of the soldiers explained. "There's a scanner in place."

"Where is it?"

The soldier pointed to the right corner of the room.

"You're up, Doc." Locke took my mom's arm and brought her over to the door.

This time, she complied without resistance and leaned her face close to the scanner. The familiar thin blue line swept across the device as it scanned my mom's eye. Moments later, the door clicked open. The armory was a long and narrow room, with a stockpile of guns, rifles, grenades, helmets, goggles, vests, and other things I couldn't identify.

Locke motioned toward the room. "Grab your gear. We need to be prepared."

In single file, the soldiers stood in line, awaiting their turn to enter. One by one, they selected items off the shelves, grabbing vests and helmets and their weapons. Locke monitored their gear, as if he were conducting inventory. The line diminished, but there were still a few soldiers still gathering their gear when a deafening explosion reverberated through the ceiling, dislodging panels and sending dust and broken plaster crashing to the floor. Before anyone could react, another blast struck, its force triggering the alarms. Instinctively, I ducked and shielded Mia with my body. "Was that a bomb or an earthquake?" I shouted.

"That was a bomb!" someone yelled. Oh, God! Was it Todd?

Locke surveyed the scene, his eyes wide. Within seconds, he was yelling into his phone, "Briggs, do you copy? Briggs?" Dead silence greeted him. His gaze narrowed as he checked his phone. "My phone's dead." He urgently waved us toward the door and shouted, "Everyone, move!"

We charged through the barrack doors and almost ran into Briggs and the doctors supporting Todd between them. He clung to their arms like crutches, wobbling unsteadily. His face was several shades of pale, and a bloodied bandage covered a section of his abdomen.

"Jesus, Briggs," Locke blurted. "Thank God you're all right." His gaze flickered on Todd's bandage. "Did you get it? Are we good?"

Briggs' eyes were as wide and wild as Locke's. "I had just defused the bomb when we heard the blast. I think it came from the lobby. I couldn't reach anyone. My cell's dead."

"Mine, too. We need to get to Gibson. Hopefully—" Before Locke could finish, another blast shuddered the building. His gaze met Briggs'. "My guess is that they're blowing up floors one at a time, and the bomb inside Todd was to detonate the basement. We need to get Gibson and get to the lobby like yesterday."

"One hundred percent. Everyone, let's move!"

The building continued to groan, sending clouds of dust swirling beneath the flickering lights as Briggs and Locke led us through the dim corridor back to the elevator and Gibson's team. The first time we made our way from the elevator to the barracks, it seemed to take forever. But, now, in reverse, or perhaps due to the chaos and panic, time flew by. Relief shuddered through me as we rounded the corner and found Gibson's team gathered in the same spot, unharmed. My gaze caught sight of the elevator. Its door was thrown wide open and dangling by cables, and the floor inside was demolished. The explosions must have derailed it. The relief I felt vanished. Without the elevator, we were screwed.

"Thank God." Gibson mumbled, and then his gaze fell on Todd. "What the hell happened here?"

"DFOG implanted a bomb in this soldier," Briggs replied. "He was given an order to detonate himself if the project was exposed." He gestured toward the doctors. "They were able to locate the bomb and remove it. Luckily, I defused it, and then the explosion hit."

Gibson's eyes widened in disbelief. "A bomb was inside you, soldier?"

"I'm okay, sir," Todd said, his voice weak.

Gibson's gaze clouded with disbelief, but he quickly shook it off and refocused on the situation. "The blasts seem to be starting on the upper floors and working their way downward. The explosions seemed to have disabled my phone. The explosions destroyed the elevator. We need to find another way out."

"We're trapped," someone muttered.

My mind raced with worst-case scenarios: suffocating in the rubble, being blown apart, or being crushed by the collapsing building. Shaking my head hard, I pushed away the dark thoughts. I had to stay positive and believe we'd find a way to make it out alive, all of us. I whispered in Mia's ear, "We'll make it." I wasn't sure if I said it more for myself or her.

She barely nodded but squeezed my hand.

"We're not trapped," Dr. Matrey spoke up. "There's an emergency stairwell opposite the elevator. We can use it to reach the lobby."

Gibson disagreed. "There's no stairwell on the plans."

"I've used it myself many times." He gestured to Dr. Blanchett. "We've all used it."

"It's true," Dr. Blanchett confirmed, "and it's our only option right now."

Gibson set his gaze on Briggs and Locke, who both nodded with their agreement. "Okay. We'll follow you. Let's move out."

The doctors maintained a hurried pace as they led us through the dim corridor. We passed battered doors, debris scattered across the floor, and more clouds of dust lingering in the air. In my head, I prayed that the stairs were still intact. Mia moaned, and a wave of panic washed over me. Her jaw was clenched and her eyelids were half-closed, clearly in pain. I held her tighter, kissed the top of her head, and gently stroked her back. I didn't know what else I could do. She rested her head against me and seemed to relax some.

Dr. Matrey slowed his stride, stopped in front of an unmarked steel door, and pressed his palm just above the handle. I didn't notice any scanner activate, but the door swung wide open, granting us access. The concrete stairwell stretched endlessly upward, with floor after floor rising before us. From what I could see, it seemed to be intact. My prayers were answered.

"Keep moving," Gibson urged, waving the doctors forward.

The doctors led the way, with Todd positioned between them, and then Gibson. I helped Mia climb each stair, wincing with her every time she gritted her teeth in pain. The soldiers followed closely behind us, while my mom, Briggs, and Locke brought up the rear. Another explosion drowned out the soldiers' combat boots pounding against the steps in the stairwell. We all stopped, hunched over, bracing for the fallout. When none came, we pressed on.

The more floors we passed and the higher we climbed, new terrifying sounds drifted toward us: screams, gunfire, and the scraping of metal, as if the building were shifting on its foundation. My pulse throbbed in my ears, racing faster and faster. I suddenly wished I could take back the offer that Mia and I made to help BSI. My grandma would never have let me come if she knew the horrors we would face, and she was right. I was just a 19-year-old guy with asthma, with no business being among super soldiers and BSI agents. But maybe, I thought, Mia needed me. For that reason, I had to believe I served a purpose on this mission and pushed myself to round each flight of stairs, with Mia at my side, until we reached the top.

The last stair led onto a landing with a door to its right. Dr. Matrey stood in front of the door, listening. The booming rumbling noises abruptly ceased, leaving an unsettling dead calm over the stairwell. "This is it," he said, glancing over his shoulder. "This door opens directly into the lobby."

Gibson motioned for him to step aside and waited for the soldiers, Briggs, and Locke to catch up. Addressing the situation, Gibson said, "Without cell phone access, we can't communicate with anyone, and SWAT should have arrived by now, but the silence coming from the other side of that door tells me differently. There could be DFOG guards waiting to ambush us, and once we open this door, we've got no protection."

My mom stepped forward and offered. "I could safely enter the lobby."

Locke sliced a rigid hand through the air. "After what you've put us through, absolutely not. You can't be trusted."

"Locke's right," Briggs agreed.

"I could go," Dr. Matrey offered. "Or at least crack the door and see what we're looking at. If there are guards, they'll recognize me."

"Crack the door," Gibson ordered.

Dr. Matrey cracked the door and peered out. He quickly shut it and faced Gibson. "The lobby's vacant."

Gibson slowly pushed the door open and stepped out of the stairwell. He reappeared and waved us forward. Briggs and Locke led the way, followed closely by the soldiers. The rest of us then stepped into what was clearly a war zone, not a lobby. Shattered glass, bullet casings, and broken furniture covered the floor. Half of the front desk was smashed, the walls were bashed in, and fluorescent lights dangled from the ceiling, flickering on and off. The rancid smell of smoke contaminated the air, making me want to gag, and I hoped it wouldn't trigger my asthma.

"Over here," one of the soldiers called out, waving Gibson over to the front desk.

Behind what was left of it lay several lifeless DFOG guards, each with a single gunshot to the head, their blood splattered around them. Colonel Bennett, my dad, Cooper, and the rest of her team were missing.

"Something feels off. I don't like it," Gibson voiced, glancing around.

A bright flash and a deafening crack erupted around us. For several seconds, the blinding flash left me disoriented, and a high-pitched ringing filled my ears. As the ringing gradually subsided, sharp bursts of gunfire erupted around us. I dropped to the ground, pulling Mia down with me. My heart raced as a bullet ricocheted off the wall above us. Gibson's voice broke through the chaos, signaling his team, "It's Bennett and several DFOG guards. Cover and return fire!"

Locke, Briggs, and the soldiers ducked into firing positions, aiming at the DFOG guards. Dr. Matrey and Dr. Blanchett shielded my mom and Todd as they dashed behind a marble column. I grabbed Mia and followed them. Crouched low behind the column, adrenaline pushed fear aside for a moment, but the chaotic battle around us quickly brought it flooding back. Gunshots and flash bombs pierced my ears and stung my eyes. Gibson, Briggs, and Locke shouted commands, but I couldn't make them out.

The front doors to the building burst open, and boots thudded against the floor, echoing through the lobby. A squad of heavily armed figures in dark uniforms surged toward the front desk in tight formation, weapons raised. Instinctively, I ducked even lower behind a column, my heart hammering so loudly I was sure everyone around me could hear. Chaos came from every direction. I couldn't think straight. I was so scared of having an asthma attack that I held my breath before I caught the bold white letters—SWAT—emblazoned across their vests, and my shoulders sank with relief.

"Federal agents! Arrest warrant! Get on the ground! Do it now!" One barked, his voice sharp and commanding.

Another repeated, "Get on the ground! Now!" His tone was even more urgent as he swept his rifle across the room, eyes narrowed behind his visor.

Silence fell over the lobby as Bennett locked eyes with the SWAT team, both sides with guns drawn, each measuring the other's resolve. Bennett's jaw tightened, his fingers flexing and unflexing around the grip of his weapon. SWAT held their position, no hint of emotion on their faces. The SWAT team took a step forward, the red lasers of their guns circling on Bennett. Within seconds, Bennett lowered his gun, placed it on the front desk, and raised his hands above his head. A grin spread across his face as a light flashed above the entrance, the strobing glow flickering over the room.

"Run!" Gibson roared.

SWAT retreated, moving with swift precision as they formed a protective wall around us, commanding, "Move!" They urged us toward the exit, their loud and urgent tones underscoring the urgency of the moment. I forced my legs to run, convinced we were fleeing from another bomb, this one alarmingly close. The walls surrounding the entrance howled with a thunderous roar, splitting away for the doors. Glass shattered, fire erupted, and the ground shook, knocking me off balance. Above the entrance, the ceiling buckled and split apart, spewing dust and concrete. Mia seized me and, with all her strength, propelled me through the hole where the doors once stood. I hit the ground hard, rolling across the pavement before scrambling to my feet and spinning around. Flames and smoke engulfed the entrance as it crumbled to the ground, sealing access to the building and enclosing Mia and many others inside.

"Mia!" I screamed, dashing forward.

"No, Ethan." Briggs yanked me back. "It's not safe." He pointed behind him. "They're here to help."

My gaze fell upon police officers, firefighters, paramedics, and their flashing emergency vehicles spread throughout the parking lot. Several officers were questioning Dr. Blanchett, Cooper, and her team. I stared at them thinking, "Thank God they got out." A few feet away, my parents sat in the back of one of the police cars. I clenched my jaw, glaring at them, not feeling a shred of sympathy. So many times, I'd wished that they'd been present in my life, cried that they weren't, and felt sorry for myself. Today wasn't one of those days. Today, I felt thankful it was my grandma who raised me and that I was nothing like my parents. Their scientific minds caused this damage, and I hoped they'd be locked up forever.

I turned my back on them and focused on the building. The heavy thud of my heartbeat hammered inside my chest as my eyes moved over the collapsed entrance. The police, firefighters, SWAT officers, Gibson, Briggs, and eleven super soldiers worked together to clear away the rubble. The soldiers acted like machines, tossing aside broken chunks of concrete like they were weightless. Without their strength, there was no chance of getting back inside.

Mia hurling me through the doors replayed in my mind. Somewhere inside, she was trapped alongside Locke, Dr. Matrey, the remaining soldiers, and the looming threat of Colonel Bennett and DFOG guards. She had to be alive. They all had to be alive. I had to hold onto that belief!

Chapter 10

I paced back and forth, watching the soldiers and first responders continue to sift through the wreckage. Their progress was frustratingly slow, even with the soldiers' strength. The firefighters, drenched in sweat, struggled to move debris with their crowbars and axes. Police officers covered in dust were pushing aside shattered masonry. Everyone was continuously cautioning us that the structure was unstable and that any further collapse would be catastrophic—just what I didn't need to hear.

The small hole they managed to make allowed me a glimpse inside the building. Bits and pieces of debris scattered across the floor. It drove me insane just standing there and doing nothing, but every time I got close to the destruction, Briggs pushed me back. Maybe he thought I wasn't strong enough, or perhaps he was worried about my asthma, or maybe he just didn't want me to see what was really inside. I wasn't sure, but what I did know was that I couldn't keep waiting. Not knowing was killing me. I needed to see Mia. I needed to know she was okay.

My cell phone buzzed in my pocket. I pulled it out and glanced at the screen, seeing it was my grandma. I answered immediately, tears flooding my eyes. "Grandma, I can't even…" I took a shaky breath. "The building. It collapsed with Mia inside!"

"Ethan," her voice was so calm. "Breathe. I know you've been through more than anyone should have to bear. Sheriff Reid has been keeping me updated. I just dropped Hank and Gracie off at Sarah and Glen's. I'm on my way to the airport now. I'll be there soon."

"Thank you," I gasped. "How long before you're here?"

"About two hours."

"Grandma, Mia has to make it. I don't know how I'll cope if…"

"Stay positive. I'm praying for her and the others. Hold on, and I'll be there soon."

"Hurry, okay?"

"I'll do my best. Love you."

"Love you, too."

She hung up, leaving me staring at my phone. A wave of helplessness washed over me, and I hung my head. Someone tapped me on my shoulder, and I looked up to see Dr. Blanchett standing in front of me.

"How are you holding up?"

I just shook my head.

She glanced at the building and then looked back at me. "I'm not making light of the situation, but only the entrance collapsed. The main lobby is still intact." She pointed to the structure, where the roof of the building was visible just beyond the front doors. "Colonel Bennett is no fool. He wouldn't set off an explosion that would endanger himself or his guards. Mia and the other soldiers are tough."

"It's just taking so long, and the longer it takes, the higher the chance that their injuries—" My asthma kicked in and cut me off. I took out my inhaler and sprayed a dose into my mouth.

"Are you okay?"

I nodded, and after a moment I said, "I have asthma. When I'm stressed, it gets worse. What I was trying to say was that their injuries would worsen. I've seen what happens to patients who weren't treated in time."

She placed her hand gently on my forearm, compassion evident in her eyes. "I'm a doctor, Ethan. I understand, but we must keep in mind that Mia and the other soldiers are hybrids, and that will save them. We have to hold onto that belief."

The sound of a car engine starting drew my attention away from Dr. Blanchett. The police car containing my parents headed toward the exit. As it turned onto the street, it quickly vanished from my view. I felt nothing and hoped I'd never lay eyes on or hear from my parents again, ever. All I needed was my grandma, Mia, and Hank and Gracie.

"It will—" A cracking, grinding reverberation cut Dr. Blanchett off. The noise came from the building, and I feared the rest of it would collapse. But what I saw was the opposite; something was erupting from it. The broken concrete slabs tumbled forward, spewing debris. Everyone quickly backed away, and Gibson raised his gun. Briggs and SWAT followed suit, aiming their weapons at the wreckage.

In the haze, there was movement. At first, just shadows, and then a soldier emerged, shoving aside a tangled mass of rebar with bleeding, dirt-streaked hands. His helmet was cracked, one eye was swollen shut, and he was coughing out dust. Behind him, another soldier clawed her way free, one arm hung limp at her side, and blood dripped from a gash in her shoulder.

"Jesus," whispered a firefighter, his grip slipping from the handle of his axe.

"Look—there's more of them!" A police officer shouted.

Through the jagged hole, Locke appeared, with a firm grip on Colonel Bennett, whose hands were cuffed behind his back. Locke's jaw was clenched, his eyes cold and unyielding as he pushed the colonel forward. Bennett's face contorted with anger as he resisted Locke's grip, struggling against him. Briggs dashed forward, clapped a hand on Locke's shoulder, and then swiftly got on the other side of Colonel Bennett, helping to lead him toward one of the cruisers.

My gaze was locked on the opening, watching, waiting, and hoping to see Mia. Another figure staggered forward, Dr. Matrey. Blood ran down the side of his head, matting his hair and dripping onto his ripped lab coat. His hand was pressed against his wound as he made his way through the rubble. Dr. Blanchett rushed to his side, wrapping her arm around him and guiding him over to the paramedics.

More soldiers followed, some crawling, some hobbling with broken limbs, dragging themselves out of the wreckage. Their dusty, torn uniforms revealed purple bruises and deep cuts on their skin smeared with blood. For several agonizing minutes, there was no movement at all, and my heart sank. A wave of panic threatened to consume me just as the soldier with gray eyes and the comic book character fought their way through the rubble, carrying Mia.

I stood frozen, my mouth hanging open in shock, then I ran, shoving past soldiers and SWAT. "M-Mia!" My voice cracked with fright as my gaze darted over her ghostly pale face streaked with dirt. The way her head hung to the side, I knew it wasn't a good sign. Blood soaked through the front of her shredded hoodie, exposing bright red pooling beneath a deep, ragged gash across her abdomen. One leg dangled limply, her joggers torn off to show a bruised, mangled mess. Her pale face, labored breaths, and the blood spilling from her wounds were all I could think about. Tears filled my eyes, but I didn't dare let them fall. I couldn't let her sense my fear, only my support. "I've got you," I whispered, brushing my hand across her cheek.

Pounding boots came from behind me before SWAT officers, paramedics, and Dr. Blanchett surrounded us. "Lay her on the ground," Dr. Blanchett ordered.

I moved backward and stood off to the side, letting the team help Mia. Crowded around her, they quickly assessed her injuries. Dr. Blanchett spoke to the paramedic next to her like she was reading a to-do list. "Abdominal laceration, extensive blood loss, and fractures to her femur and tibia on the left leg."

He hooked Mia up to a monitor, placed a dressing over her abdomen, and applied pressure, rattling off her vitals, "BP 90/60, heart rate 118."

Dr. Blanchett and one of the SWAT officers were quietly talking to each other. I had to lean forward and strain to hear their conversation. I caught the end of what the SWAT officer said, "There's internal bleeding. She needs immediate transfer to a hospital for surgical evaluation."

"She's crashing!" Dr. Blanchett exclaimed as she quickly started CPR.

The paramedic next to her grabbed the defibrillator and began charging it.

A sickening feeling landed in my gut as I shouted, "What's happening?"

Placing the defibrillator on Mia's chest, the paramedic shouted, "Clear!"

Everyone moved back before the machine automatically shocked Mia.

I couldn't tear my gaze away from the monitor as I held my breath. When a steady rhythm began to beep, I gasped and slumped forward, resting my hands on my knees. One of the paramedics scrambled to his feet and raced to his vehicle. Within seconds, the ambulance came screeching to a stop in front of us. The two paramedics treating Mia lifted her off the ground and laid her on the stretcher inside the van. Dr. Blanchett climbed in next, and I followed. I scooted over to the far corner to get out of their way. Everyone huddled over Mia, and I couldn't see what was happening, but she had to know I was there, so I said, "I'm here, Mia. I won't leave you."

The paramedic behind the wheel pulled away and headed out of the parking lot, alarm blaring and lights flashing. One of the two paramedics working on Mia started speaking into a radio. "Jade Forest Hospital, this is Rescue 3, and we are en route. We have an 18-year-old female with severe traumatic injuries—a deep abdominal laceration, significant blood loss, and fractures to her left leg. The patient suffered a cardiac arrest on scene. CPR was initiated and one round of defibrillation administered. Return of spontaneous circulation was achieved after approximately two minutes.

"Currently, the patient is unconscious but has a steady pulse. Blood pressure is 90/60, heart rate 118, respirations spontaneous, and oxygen saturation 96 percent on room air. Two large-bore IVs in place with fluids running. ETA is five minutes. Requesting trauma team and surgical standby."

"Rescue 3, this is Jade Forest Hospital," said a woman's voice came over the speaker. "Copy your report on the 18-year-old female, severe trauma, post-cardiac arrest, ROSC achieved, and current vitals. Trauma and surgical teams have been notified and are preparing for immediate receipt. Continue monitoring vitals and notify us of any changes en route. Proceed directly to Trauma Bay 1 on arrival."

"Jade Forest Hospital, Rescue 3 copies. Continuing monitoring and will advise of any changes. ETA is now four minutes. Proceeding directly to Trauma Bay 1. Rescue 3 out."

Those four minutes felt like four hours before the ambulance rolled into Trauma Bay 1, the first of five designated spots by the hospital's emergency entrance. Waiting for us in green scrubs were two men and three women standing outside the hospital's emergency automatic doors. The intensity of their faces reminded me of my grandma when she knew she was walking into a life-threatening case. The ambulance doors swung open, and the paramedics jumped out. Someone said, "On my count, 1, 2, 3."

It seemed like everyone rushed to grab the stretcher and pull it out of the ambulance at once. The paramedics adjusted the stretcher height and placed the monitor, an IV bag, and a blood bag next to Mia on the top of the stretcher. Voices blended together as they wheeled Mia into the entrance, with the paramedic shouting out new vitals and rehashing her injuries. The trauma team quickly took charge, maneuvering the stretcher down the hallway toward the double doors. One of the men, his temples grayed with age, held us back. "I'm sorry, but you will need to wait in the lobby. We will provide information as soon as we can."

"You don't understand this patient's unique circumstances." Dr. Blanchett disagreed. "Her anatomy is unlike anything you've encountered before. She is a military super soldier. Please allow me to accompany you."

A dazed expression settled on his wrinkled forehead as he stood there, staring for several seconds before finally waving them forward. Dr. Blanchett placed her hand on my shoulder and reassured me, "I promise you, I will do everything possible to save her." With that, she hurried away and disappeared behind the double doors, leaving me alone in the hallway.

With my choices taken away from me, the only thing I could do was wait in the lobby. Before heading there, I texted my grandma and gave her the name and address of the hospital. I didn't get a reply, but she was probably on the plane. As I turned toward the lobby, the emergency doors reopened, bringing in Dr. Matrey and the remaining injured soldiers on stretchers. Briggs and Locke were also there, although they didn't need treatment. Briggs and Locke came straight toward me. Locke gripped my shoulder as he asked, "What's Mia's status? Do they know?"

I shook my head. "They just took her back. Dr. Blanchett is with them."

Briggs rested his hand on my shoulder and offered, "She's in good hands."

"They asked me to wait in the lobby."

"We'll wait with you."

Walking down the hallway away in silence, we pushed through the emergency doors and entered the lobby. Rows of chairs and side tables filled the room with people on their phones or drinking coffee, waiting on news about a family member, a loved one, or maybe a friend. A coffee station occupied the far corner next to a small refrigerator stocked with bottled water. Plants were scattered about, and colorful paintings hung on the walls. Plants and paintings weren't going to soften the atmosphere. Everyone knew why they were there, and nothing was going to change that.

I sank into one of the seats and clasped my hands, becoming just another person waiting for news. Briggs paced back and forth, seemingly unable to settle, his gaze continually darting to the emergency doors. Locke remained standing, arms crossed over his chest, his jaw set as he stared straight ahead. The clock on the wall read 11:20 p.m., but that couldn't be right. Hadn't it been just moments ago that Mia and I walked into the DFOG building? Everything seemed to have happened in the blink of an eye, yet somehow, a whole day had passed. Laying my head against the chair, I sank deeper, closing my eyes.

"Ethan!"

Hearing my name shouted jolted me to my feet. I turned toward the voice and saw Dr. Blanchett frantically waving me forward.

"Ethan, come quick. We need you!"

I rushed toward her. "What is it? Is Mia okay?"

Briggs and Locke followed closely behind. Dr. Blanchett held them back. "They're only allowing Ethan into the trauma room."

Over my shoulder, I called out to Briggs and Locke. "My grandma is coming to the hospital.

Can you please keep an eye out for her?" Without waiting for a response, I rushed through the emergency doors, following Dr. Blanchett. "You didn't answer me. Is she okay?"

"She regained consciousness but is hysterical. She hasn't stopped asking for you, and we can't seem to calm her down. I'm concerned about the impact on her injuries."

I knew immediately the cause of Mia's mistrust. It was fear of being overpowered and losing her control once more.

As we approached the open door, shouting, metal clanging, and machines beeping filled the hallway. I ran, skidding to a stop just inside the doorway. The medical staff stood in the middle of the room, looking bewildered. Bloody towels and IV bags spilling crimson red and clear fluid cluttered the white floor. Mia had yanked out both her IVs, and blood trickled down her arms. Her eyes held a wild, animalistic sheen that shifted between gold and turquoise. Sweat covered her, and her breaths were ragged. Clutching the guardrail on the gurney, she screamed, "Stay away! Where's Ethan? I want Ethan!"

A woman nurse or doctor, I couldn't tell which, had her hands outstretched, and in a gentle voice, she said, "Mia, please, let us help you."

"No!" she screamed. "Don't touch me!"

Goosebumps scurried down my arms, but I couldn't freak out, not now. Mia was terrified, resisting, and losing blood fast. I forced myself to remain calm as I said, "Mia, I'm here. It's going to be okay. I won't let anything happen to you."

Her head snapped in my direction, and the wild panic in her eyes shifted to recognition. Her entire body sagged against the bed. "Ethan," she gasped, reaching for me.

I was at her bedside in two strides and took hold of her hand, squeezing tight. "I'm here, Mia."

"I didn't give them permission to put anything into my body." She pointed to the mess on the floor. "I pulled out the IVs. Now, they're saying I need surgery. I don't trust them."

"Mia, these people are not DFOG. They work at this hospital, and their only agenda is to save your life." I kept my voice soft but emphasized my words. "Look at your stomach. Look at your leg. The building collapsed on top of you. You need the fluids, the blood, and the surgery."

Her eyes searched mine, and I hoped she could see the truth in them. After a few tense moments, she said, "No anesthesia. I have to be awake."

I shook my head firmly. "No, Mia. Not this time. The pain would be unbearable without anesthesia." I squeezed her hands and pressed them against my chest. "Look at me, Mia. I wouldn't lie to you. You know that. I'm scared right now. I can't lose you. You have to let them do what they need to do to save your life!"

Tears flooded her eyes and rolled down her cheeks, but she never looked away from me. "Then you have to be in the room with me. You have to be my voice."

I faced the team of five, unsure of who were doctors and who were nurses, so I directed my questions to all of them. "Is that an option? Can I be in the OR while she's having surgery?"

The woman with brown hair piled on top of her head and the shortest of the team shook her head. "It's against hospital policy."

The man with olive skin suggested, "We could allow him to sit in the operating theater."

They all just stared at each other for a moment. It was the tallest woman on the team that finally said, "Please show him and Dr. Blanchett to the operating theater."

The man gestured toward the door, but before I left, I leaned over Mia, placing my lips on hers and kissing her softly. "Everything will be okay. I'll be watching."

She clung to me for a moment, her shoulders quaking. "You're my voice, Ethan." Then she released me.

I nodded and forced myself to exit the room, following the man with olive skin. "I need to stop in the lobby," I said. "My grandma is coming to the hospital. She's also a doctor. Also, there are two BSI agents that I need to update."

The man gestured to himself and said, "I'm Nurse Bailey. I'll be showing you to the theater, but yes, we can stop in the lobby first."

"Are you or the others part of the surgical team?" Dr. Blanchett asked.

"Yes, along with our trauma surgeon, Dr. Ellis, and our orthopedic surgeon, Dr. Holt. They will be taking over the case. Mia will be in excellent hands."

"We'll need to brief him on her anatomy and blood type."

Great, more doctors I hadn't met. I hoped Mia wouldn't freak out, or I'd be rushing into the operation room to calm her down again.

"They're both highly skilled, but given Mia's unique situation, they may have questions for you. If so, they can address it from the theater."

"Very well."

We reached the lobby doors, and I stepped through first, scanning the room for my grandma or Briggs and Locke. When I spotted my grandma's caramel-brown hair, my knees weakened. I quickly steadied myself and rushed toward her. She enfolded me in her arms, and I clung to her, unable to suppress the fear I had been hiding about Mia's injuries. I cried as she softly stroked my back, murmuring, "She'll be all right."

Wiping tears from my face, I managed to pull myself together. Releasing her, I gestured to people around me and said, "It looks like you met Agent Briggs and Agent Locke. This is Dr. Blanchett from DFOG and Nurse Bailey from the hospital." Then I pointed at my grandma. "This is my grandma, Dr. Evelyn Porter."

After everyone shook hands, I said, "Mia's going into surgery. She wanted me with her, but that wasn't possible, so Nurse Bailey is taking me to the operating theater." I turned to Nurse Bailey and added, "I'm assuming we can all go."

He glanced at everyone's tense faces before finally nodding. "Please follow me," he said, then turned and walked toward the lobby doors.

***

The operating theater was exactly that. There were three elevated rows of seats, with ten chairs to a row. They faced a large glass window that looked down on the operating room. The bright lights make the room look even colder and more intimidating. Several people in green scrubs wearing masks and gloves were already in the room setting things up. They looked up as we filed in, taking seats in the front row. Briggs and Locke were at the right end, followed by Dr. Blanchett, my grandma, and then me. A male doctor stepped forward and introduced himself. "Hello, I'm Dr. Ellis." He nodded to the right. "This is Dr. Holt."

Dr. Holt raised his hand to identify himself.

"About her blood type," Dr. Ellis continued, "we don't store DEA 1.1 negative. I could ask one of the closest veterinarians for it, but I'm not sure if there's time. Can we use her O positive blood type for the transfusion?"

Dr. Blanchett shook her head, but before she could say anything, I leaned over and said, "They brought in several super soldiers after we arrived. One of them might have the right blood type."

"Do you remember their names or what they looked like?"

I didn't know many of the soldiers, but I definitely recognized four of them. I felt odd about telling her the nicknames I gave them so I could keep them straight in my head. Given the urgency of the situation, I just blurted out, "A guy with gray eyes, another guy who looks like a comic book superhero, a girl with freakish-looking eyes, and another girl with braids."

"Perfect." She stood up and introduced herself. "I'm Dr. Blanchett from DFOG. You may have the blood type on site. Several other super soldiers were brought in through emergency, and two are an exact match for Mia's blood type. Their names are Piper Mathews and Colby Durham."

He quickly turned to someone in the room. The man picked up a phone mounted on the wall, spoke for a moment, then hung up. Turning back to Dr. Ellis, he said, "Both are still here and will be donating blood for Mia."

The OR doors swung open, and Mia was wheeled in on a gurney. She immediately looked up at the window. I stood up, waved, and reassured her, "I'm here."

A faint smile came to her lips as she waved back.

My stomach twisted into knots as Dr. Ellis and Dr. Holt reviewed her chart, conveniently discussing their plan in hushed voices so I couldn't hear. My focus switched to the anesthesiologist sitting by Mia's head, checking her IV and monitors. "Hi Mia, I'm Dr. Patel, your anesthesiologist. I'm going to give you some medicine through your IV. You might notice a cool sensation in your arm. That's completely normal."

He placed a mask over her nose and mouth. "I need you to breathe in and take slow, deep breaths for me. You'll start to feel very relaxed and sleepy. If you notice a little dizziness, that's just the medicine working. You're doing great." He glanced at the monitors, giving Mia a nod. "In a few seconds, you'll drift off, and when you wake up, your surgery will be done. We'll take good care of you the whole time."

As I watched from the other side of the glass, I caught Mia looking at me. Her hand flexed slightly as the medication flowed through her IV. I smiled at her, though she may not have seen it as her eyelids grew heavy and she slipped into an unconscious state. The sounds of the operating room were muffled and distant as a wave of helplessness washed over me. It was now in the hands of the doctors, and I had to remind myself that I was Mia's advocate. Surgical drapes covered her stomach and left leg, and her skin was prepared for the procedure. The bright overhead lights glinted off the scalpels arranged on the tray beside the operating table.

"We need that blood," Dr. Ellis stated. "Can someone get an ETA?"

A woman nodded and quickly removed her gloves before using the phone. Ending the call, she snapped new gloves onto her hands as she said, "It's on its way."

In no more than a few minutes, the OR doors opened again, and a staff member wearing scrubs, a mask, and gloves wheeled in a cart housing four bags of blood. A member of the surgical team took the cart from them, and the staff member quickly exited the OR. The man swiftly connected the blood bag to Mia's IV, after which Dr. Ellis and Dr. Holt began surgery. I looked away as their scalpels pressed against her flesh. My grandma squeezed my hand and whispered, "She'll be okay."

I hadn't gotten a chance to talk to my grandma and see how she felt about my dad and his role in this mess, not to mention his arrest. I'd cut ties with my parents years ago, but he was her son. How does a parent react when their child has committed a crime, inflicted harm, and lied? But hadn't I also played a role in this? Mia was lying on an OR table, having emergency surgery because she threw me out of a collapsing building. She'd had her DNA altered by my parents, changing her and many others into hybrids so the military could exploit them for power. These soldiers were stripped of their rights, imprisoned, manipulated, tortured, and forced to fight someone else's battle. And even with everything Mia had gone through, her nature was to be kind, caring, and a genuine person. I was lucky to be the person she cared for. I had to tell her how much she meant to me as soon as she got out of surgery and was recovering.

"Joann, I need more blood. There's a bleeder."

Hearing Dr. Ellis's words, I jerked my head upright and centered on Mia. Blood pooled around her abdomen, and Dr. Ellis's hands were deep inside her, searching for the source. Helplessness crashed over me, and it tightened around my chest like a fist. "No! I won't have an episode. Not now. I'm her voice!" I screamed in my head. I opened my mouth to say something, anything, but Joann quickly replaced the blood bag, and Dr. Ellis was doing everything he could.

My grandma squeezed my hand again. "Breathe, Ethan."

"Found it," Dr. Ellis announced, pressing gauze into Mia's abdomen, but the blood kept welling up, refusing to slow. "It's coming from her spleen. It's ruptured." His gaze flicked to the monitor. "Her pressure's dropping. It needs to come out."

Once more, I lowered my eyes and clasped my hands in my lap to keep them from trembling. The constant beeping of the monitor gave me the strength I needed to calm my lungs.

"Extracting," Dr. Ellis's voice, along with the metallic clicks of surgical instruments, filled my ears. "Okay. Looks good. Let's irrigate and check for any more bleeders."

"She's not out of danger yet," Dr. Holt chimed in. "Her femur and tibia are shattered. The rods and plates aren't holding. I have to amputate."

"No!" I shouted, springing from my seat. "She wouldn't want that. You have to save her leg!"

Dr. Blanchett ejected from her seat as well, stepping up to the glass and joining me and fighting for Mia. "Losing her spleen is one thing. Her leg is another. Give her regenerative abilities a chance."

Dr. Holt's hands hovered over Mia as he hesitated, and then he shook his head. "I don't live in that world, Dr. Blan—"

A sudden, sharp pop echoed from Mia's leg, cutting him off. His eyes darted downward. We all saw what he had. Two broken bones in Mia's leg snapped together like connecting puzzle pieces, the surrounding tissues knitting closed.

Dr. Blanchett gasped and clapped her hands, shouting. "See! Her body is trying to heal itself. You can't amputate."

"Damn," Locke mumbled. "Mia is one badass soldier."

The surgical team gawked at the phenomenon before them, pausing with awe and disbelief. "All right then," Dr. Holt stated with a curt nod. "Continuing with stabilization." His focus returned to piecing her bones together with the hardware.

For the first time, hope surged inside me; though it was fragile, I felt it grow with each beat of my heart.

CHAPTER 11

S itting next to Mia in the recovery room, I held her hand and gazed at her. To me, her strawberry blonde hair was again a tangled mess lying against the white pillow, yet she looked beautiful. The rose-pink flush had returned to her cheeks, lying underneath all her freckles. The desire to kiss her burned on my lips, but I hesitated to wake her. She had endured so much, and she looked so serene as she peacefully slept. I just couldn't bring myself to disturb her.

I desperately needed a shower, but I wanted Mia to find me sitting next to her when she opened her eyes. Briggs and Locke had dropped off our overnight bags, so I at least had the chance to change my clothes. Grandma had booked us a hotel room, and she had already stopped by the hospital twice to bring me breakfast and lunch. Sarah had texted me a few pictures of Hank and Gracie. They looked like they were having a blast riding in Glen's snowplow truck and helping him clear the roads, and Sarah was showering them with treats. Everything seemed to be coming together, but that was only within the limited confines of the recovery room with Mia.

When Briggs and Locke brought our bags, they filled me in on the situation at DFOG. The entire building had been evacuated. My parents, Colonel Bennett, and several captains, including Mia's captain, along with the DFOG guards, were facing federal charges. It was also possible that doctors Blanchett and Matrey could be in danger as well, though if they cooperated and provided critical information, Briggs said they could be granted immunity. I, Mia, and the other soldiers were considered witnesses, and we'd have to provide our statements at some point, implying that this thing was far from over. But I'd deal with all of that once Mia was better. Everything else beyond these hospital walls could wait. The small space of the recovery room and the rhythmic hum of machines pushed away my thoughts, and I waited for the moment when Mia would open her eyes. When she did, she would find me there.

I continued to sit quietly by her bedside, my hand still wrapped around hers, watching the rise and fall of her chest and the soft beeping of the monitors. I'd drawn the curtain, separating her from the other bed and adding a bit of privacy.

She moaned, stirring awake and slowly opening her eyes. They appeared unfocused, searching the room for answers. For a brief second confusion flickered across her face, but as her gaze settled on me and recognition dawned, she weakly squeezed my hand.

"Hey," I said softly. "You're safe. I'm right here."

She blinked and licked her dry lips. "Ethan?" Her voice was barely more than a whisper. "You're here."

I nodded, smiling at her. "Of course. I promised you I wouldn't leave."

A faint smile appeared on her face as her eyelids fluttered closed for a moment. "I'm happy you're here," she breathed. "I knew you would be."

"How's the pain? Do you need more medicine?"

She shook her head. "Just you."

I leaned in to kiss her, and as I pulled away, I said, "Mia, I was terrified. When the building collapsed, I thought I lost you." I shuddered at the memory. "I really care about you. I've never felt this way about anyone before."

She tried to squeeze my hand. "I care about you, too, so much I can't breathe sometimes."

I laughed. "I feel the same way, and it has nothing to do with my asthma." I was about to kiss her again, but a nurse came over to check her vitals.

"I have some good news for you, Mia. We're going to transfer you to a private room. You have many visitors eager to see you, and I'm sure they'll be excited to visit with you. In a few minutes, another nurse and I will return to assist you in settling into your new room." After she left, I looked at Mia. She didn't look happy. "What's wrong, Mia?"

"I thought she was going to tell me I could go home."

I nodded, now understanding her disappointment. "From my experience with my grandma's patients, they usually want you to be able to be walking on your own before they release you. Don't worry, though. You're tough. I'm sure you'll be walking in no time. Plus, I'll be here." I got a whiff of my body and curled my lips. "Though, I really need to stop by the hotel and grab a quick shower."

"I totally get it. I'd love to take a shower too."

"Once you're in your room, ask our nurse for a bed bath and a shampoo cap."

She giggled. "Are you sure that's what it's called?"

"Yes, Mia. My grandma's a doctor, remember?"

"Okay, I'll ask them."

The sound of wheels rolling across the polished tile drew closer, accompanied by two nurses. I stood outside the doorway, shoving my hands into my pockets, while the two nurses coordinated their efforts, gently lifting Mia from the hospital bed onto the wheelchair. I caught Mia grimacing, and she tried to hide her pain with a half-smile when our eyes met. After locking the IV pole into place on the wheelchair, the nurse said, "We're all set."

I followed behind as the nurses wheeled Mia down the hallway toward the elevator, an occasional squeak of the chair filling the corridor. The other nurse hurried ahead and pushed the call button. We waited for a few seconds before the door slid open. We were heading only one floor down. I kept my eyes on Mia, searching her face for any signs of discomfort. She noticed me watching her and smiled. The elevator chimed, and the doors opened into a much quieter and less stressful environment—no multiple machines beeping in unison, or nurses and doctors running about, or that horrible sterile smell. I breathed a sigh of relief.

The nurses walked a short distance and then stopped in front of room 427. Mia's new room. The private room was brighter and quieter than the ICU. It had a single bed next to a big window, and sunlight streamed across the room, bringing a little bit of the outside in.

"Okay, Mia, we're going to transfer you onto the bed."

Mia nodded.

Together, the nurses supported her, lifting her just enough to ease her onto the bed. She winced and clenched her jaw, but once she was settled in bed and the nurses adjusted her pillows and smoothed the blanket over her, she let out a sigh and sank into the pillows. One nurse unhooked the IV bag from the chair and attached it to the pole beside the bed, checking the line. The familiar beep of the monitor was softer and less intrusive than all the beeping in the ICU.

"If you need anything," the nurse picked up the call button by the side of the bed, "just press this button, and we'll be right here." She smiled at Mia, and she and the other nurse quietly left the room.

Mia's eyes drifted around her new room, but I didn't get a chance to see how she felt before several soldiers, Briggs, and Locke filed into the room. A few had flowers, and two of them carried plants. Briggs and Locke held the biggest card I'd ever seen, full of get-well wishes. Mia's face beamed with delight. She definitely needed this, and with all these people surrounding her, it gave me the opportunity to break away and head to the hotel.

I kissed her cheek and said, "I'm going to run to the hotel while you visit with your buddies. I'll be back shortly."

She couldn't stop smiling as she nodded, waved at me, and then turned her attention to her visitors.

***

Our hotel was conveniently across the street from the hospital. It took me about five minutes to leave the hospital lobby and jog across the street to the hotel. Our hotel room was pretty cool. Grandma made sure we would have something similar to home. We had a sitting area, a small kitchen, and two separate bedrooms, each with its own bathroom.

In my room, I changed out of my smelly clothes and stepped into the shower. As showers go, this one was exceptional. Washing away the lingering odor, lathering my hair with shampoo, and shaving the five o'clock shadow across my jaw felt incredible. Stepping out of the shower and wrapping a towel around myself, I grabbed a pair of jeans, a tan long-sleeved T-shirt, and my sneakers. All my dirty clothes, I tossed into the hotel laundry bag to leave outside the door for the staff to pick up. Just as I opened my bedroom door, I spotted my grandma entering the hotel room carrying to-go containers and making her way into the sitting room. I rushed over to help her, taking the to-go containers and placing them on the table by the window

"Ethan, I'm surprised to see you here. I thought I would be delivering dinner to you at the hospital. Is Mia okay?"

"She's good. She just got transferred to a private room. A bunch of soldiers, including Briggs and Locke, stopped by, so I came here for a quick shower and a change of clothes. Speaking of which," I said, holding up my finger as I grabbed the hotel laundry bag and set it outside the door. "I'm running out of clothes. I didn't think we'd be here this long." I glanced at the to-go containers. "What's for dinner?"

"Greek salad, toasted flatbread, and iced tea."

I rubbed my stomach. "Sounds great."

We sat across from each other at the table, our to-go containers opened in front of us, using plastic utensils and sipping bottled iced tea. For several minutes, we sat together, enjoying our meal together without speaking. Finally, I broke the silence and asked, "How long do you think

Mia will be in the hospital? Do you think she'll need physical therapy, or will she be able to heal herself? What do you think?"

"I'm only making assumptions here, but considering how quickly her body heals, I don't think she'll need physical therapy or be hospitalized for long." She paused and looked at me. "But what you're forgetting, Ethan, is she's a primary witness to a federal case with multiple charges. That could extend her stay, and it affects you and me too, since we're indirectly involved."

I leaned back in my seat and groaned. "You're right, I didn't think of that." I sighed again. "God, we could be stuck here forever."

Sadness filled her eyes as she reached for my hand. "Ethan, I'm sorry my son wasn't a better father to you."

"Don't do that." I firmly shook my head. "Don't apologize for him." I squeezed her hand in a gesture to show I cared. "You didn't do this, Grandma. My parents did. Science was their life, and I was second, born with a defect. Their egos couldn't handle having a sick kid, and they became obsessed with finding a cure, but I didn't need a cure. I needed them, and they failed. Grandma, you gave me everything I could want, and I love you more than anything."

Tears filled my grandma's eyes as she wrapped her arms around me. "Oh, my sweet boy,"
she murmured. "I'm so proud of you, and I'll always be here for you."

***

Two hours later, I left the hotel and made my way back to the hospital. I stopped by the gift shop and picked up a present for Mia. I found a stuffed wolf that resembled Hank and couldn't resist buying it for her. I thought she'd really love it.

Riding the elevator to the fourth floor, I couldn't help but smile as I stared down at the stuffed wolf. I planned to hide it behind my back before entering her room to surprise her. The elevator chimed as it reached the fourth floor, and the doors slid open. I could hardly wait to see her and quickened my pace. Approaching her room number, I hid the wolf behind my back and stepped through the doorway, only to find an empty bed. The bathroom door was open and empty as well. Where was she?

Panic hit, and I struggled to catch my breath. Clutching the stuffed wolf with one hand, I reached into my pocket with the other, fumbling for my inhaler. As my fingers grasped it, I quickly pulled it out and filled my mouth with the medication. For a moment, I stood still, waiting. Gradually, one breath at a time, the tightness lessened, and without hesitating a moment longer, I ran out into the hallway.

"Are you Ethan?" a woman asked.

I spun around, searching for the voice. A nurse behind her station waved me over. I quickly dashed toward her and asked, "Did something happen? Is Mia okay?"

"She's fine. I'm sorry. I didn't mean to worry you. She asked me to keep an eye out for you. She's in imaging."

"Imaging?" I asked, my concern growing. "Did something happen?" I asked again.

"Mia insisted she's ready to start walking short distances. We were hesitant to agree since she just came from the ICU. Before making a decision, her doctors wanted to review images of her injuries to see how they are progressing. She should be back shortly."

I laid my hand over my chest, feeling my heartbeat relax. "Thank you for letting me know."

"Of course." She glanced at a monitor at her station. "Will you excuse me? I need to check on a patient."

I nodded, watching her disappear down the long hallway, and then glanced down at my hand still clinging to the stuffed wolf and laughed.

"Ethan," Mia called out.

I scanned the hallway and spotted her slowly approaching me on crutches, her left leg showing a subtle limp. A nurse walked alongside her, wheeling Mia's IV stand.

I jogged toward her, holding up the stuffed wolf.

"Oh, how cute! That looks like Hank," she said, laughing.

I kissed her softly and handed her the stuffed wolf. "That's why I got him for you."

A wide smile brightened her face as she hugged the stuffed wolf like he was really Hank.

I looked at the nurse. "Is it okay if I take over?"

She nodded and stepped aside.

I took hold of Mia's IV stand and slowed my pace to match Mia's as we headed back to her room. "You're walking. That's great!"

"I knew I was ready, but the doctors didn't believe me." She smirked. "Now they do. Next I'm going to push to go home."

I dreaded mentioning DFOG. I had forgotten about them until my grandma reminded me, and it seemed Mia had forgotten too. Going home would have to wait, but how did I gently bring that up?

"You've got that look on your face. What's up?"

"What look?"

"The one where you squish your eyebrows together."

"Hmm."

We reached her room, and after helping her settle back into bed and securing the IV stand, I pulled the chair closer to her bedside. Then I said, "So, about my look," gesturing with my fingers to indicate quotation marks, "it's because we'll probably be staying in Dencester for a while longer. We have to give our statements to BSI, remember, and you're like a main witness."

She slumped against the pillows and let out a frustrated huff. "Hasn't DFOG ruined my life enough?"

I laid my hand on her arm and said, "I'm sorry."

She brought my hand to her lips and kissed it. "You don't need to apologize. We're both stuck in this mess. I just want to be a regular person."

A knock on the door interrupted me, pulling my attention to the doorway where Gibson and Cooper stood. Mia and I exchanged glances. An eerie feeling crept under my skin to have just been discussing the topic, and they suddenly showed up. But it was no surprise; we both knew this conversation was coming.

Gibson stepped inside first and looked over at Mia. "How are you feeling, Mia?"

"We understand that you've been through a great deal," Cooper said, her tone more sympathetic than Gibson's.

Mia managed to smile. "I'm okay, thanks."

Gibson didn't waste time and got straight to the point. "Mia, Ethan, the Bureau needs both of you to come in and provide full accounts of what you know about DFOG."

"Mia, everything you endured, the abduction, the experiments," Cooper emphasized, "and all that you went through as part of their hybrid experiment is critical." She then shifted her focus to me. "And, Ethan, your insights about your experiences at DFOG, particularly concerning your parents, will be invaluable. We've also reached out to your grandmother to come in and provide her statement."

"I want to point out that a military officer will be present during the interviews," Gibson explained, "but the officer is there to only observe." Gibson gestured to Mia. "We'll work around your recovery, Mia. Just let us know when, and we'll arrange everything, including transportation."

Mia looked at me, and I took her hand.

"We'll be in touch as soon as Mia is feeling up to it," I said, my tone firm and final.

They both nodded in agreement, and Gibson added, "We'll be waiting to hear from you."

CHAPTER 12

A week and a half later, we found ourselves in the back of a black SUV, with Gibson driving us to BSI headquarters. My grandma sat to my left, and Mia was on my right. I couldn't help but keep an eye on Mia. She had only been out of the hospital for four days, and although her body had healed quickly thanks to her abilities, I noticed subtle signs that she was still experiencing discomfort.

After about ten minutes, she nudged my side and whispered, "Quit staring at me. It's making me feel self-conscious."

"I can't help it," I whispered back. "I'm concerned about you. I get that BSI wants our statements, but you should be resting back at the hotel."

"The sooner we get these statements over with, the sooner we can go home."

My grandma, clearly overhearing our conversation, paid us no attention as she focused on her phone, texting someone—most likely Dr. Jacobs, who had been filling in for her and seeing her patients at the clinic.

I shifted my attention back to Mia, who seemed convinced that giving her statement would free her from any additional responsibilities. I wanted to explain that her statement was merely the start of a long process and that a trial could stretch on for months or even years, but

I couldn't bring myself to say it. Instead, I chose to remain silent and focused my gaze out the window.

The snow had melted, signaling the arrival of spring. Sunlight filtered through the tinted windows, illuminating the pale blue sky speckled with white clouds. It made me think of Hank and Gracie. They were going to miss winter. It was their favorite time, and they loved trotting along in the snow and taking in all the scents. With all the chaos behind us and my mind at ease, I really was missing my wolves. They were such a big part of my life, and I'd never left them before. They probably wondered what happened to me, and I hoped they didn't think I had abandoned them. Sarah was definitely keeping me updated with text messages and photos, but I could hardly wait to be there in person and hear their howls and whines and feel their sloppy kisses on my face.

Mia rested her head on my shoulder and wrapped her arm beneath mine. I leaned into her, lacing our fingers together. The thought that she needed to rest crossed my mind again, but I kept it to myself. Sometimes, people just needed comfort without words.

Gibson slowed the SUV and turned into a parking garage next to a beige building with multiple floors, many windows, and two American flags hanging above its front doors. He drove upward, passing the first and second levels, and parked on the third floor next to an elevator. Just as he parked the SUV, the elevator door opened. Cooper was inside, waving us forward. We hurried over and slipped inside just as the door began to close.

Cooper pressed the fourth floor, faced Mia, my grandma, and me, and began explaining the process. "Gibson and I will be conducting your interviews. We'll each have a military officer with us to observe. You'll each be in separate interview rooms, and your interviews will be recorded. Remember, it's crucial that you share everything, no matter how insignificant you think it might be. We'll go over all of the process again once we're inside the interview room." She focused on Mia. "How's the pain, Mia?"

Mia looked at me for a second before she spoke. "It's still a little painful, but I'm doing better. Thank you for asking."

I smiled at her. At least she was truthful.

The elevator chimed, signaling that we had reached the fourth floor, and the door slid open. Cooper and Gibson walked ahead down a long, narrow hallway lined with numerous doors. The overhead lights gleamed on the polished floors, drawing attention to the tiny specks embedded in the tile. They stopped at a door in the middle of the hallway. Gibson pulled the door open and said, "Dr. Porter, this is your interview room."

Before my grandma stepped into the room, she glanced back at me and Mia. "Don't be nervous. You'll both do great."

Gibson and Cooper continued down the hallway, passing three more doors before stopping again. "Mia, this is your room," Gibson said.

Mia hugged me tightly, and as she pulled away, she added, "I'll see you soon."

I waved and then followed Gibson and Cooper to my room, which was four doors away from Mia's.

The room was entirely different from what I had expected. It wasn't like the TV shows and movies, with the scary two-way mirror in a cold, impersonal room. Instead, there was a relaxed vibe, with carpeted floors and comfortable chairs arranged around a circular table. A coffee station was set up on the counter against the back wall, and a small refrigerator was stocked with bottled water and sodas.

"Have a seat. Help yourself to some coffee, water, or soda. One of us will be back shortly."

I grabbed a Coke from the refrigerator and settled into one of the chairs, my mind racing with what I wanted to say. It didn't seem necessary to mention the whole abandonment issue with my parents; that drama felt irrelevant. I thought starting with Hank and Gracie picking up on Mia's scent would be a good beginning, but I wasn't sure how much detail to provide. They asked us to share everything, no matter how small, but some stuff was just TMI, and I really didn't want to go through everything again, even if it was just recounting. Honestly, I was glad that the whole mess was almost over.

Sitting there, I continued to run through my statements, but after twenty minutes, boredom had set in. Clearly, my interview was last since neither Cooper nor Gibson had arrived. I couldn't help but wonder what was taking so long with Mia's or my grandma's interviews. The truth was, I had no idea how long these types of things typically lasted, having never participated in one before. Feeling restless, I got up to stretch my legs and began pacing the room. The thought of stepping into the hallway and exploring crossed my mind, but I shook it off. Probably wasn't the best idea to roam around a BSI building by myself. Returning to my seat and slouching in the chair, I drummed my fingers on the table.

A creaking sound came from the door as Cooper entered alongside a man clad in a dark green uniform. His coat had silver bars across the shoulders, and badges and ribbons decorated the area above his left pocket.

"Thanks for being patient, Ethan," Cooper said before sitting down. She gestured to the man who remained standing. "This is Captain Rucker. He will be observing our interview, which is being recorded."

He nodded with a stern expression and remained silent. I got the impression he wasn't the friendly type.

"Are you ready to begin, Ethan?" Cooper asked.

Inside my head, I thought, *Really? I've been ready and waiting for you.* Out loud, I said, "Yes, I'm ready."

"This is BSI Agent Aurora Cooper, badge number 63790, conducting an official investigation of the Defense Forces of Genesis, DFOG. Can you please state your full name, date of birth, address, and that you are voluntarily cooperating with this interview?"

"My name is Ethan Jared Porter, my date of birth is May 15th, 2004, and my address is 254 Elmwood Lane, Doford Peaks, Oakridge, 96163, and yes, I volunteered to be interviewed."

"Can you state your relationship with Dr. Garrison Porter, Dr. Jade Owen, and Dr. Evelyn Porter?"

Confirming that they were my parents turned my stomach, but I had to do it. "Dr. Garrison Porter is my father. Dr. Jade Owen is my mother, and Dr. Evelyn Porter is my grandma."

"And Mia Rowe, what is your relationship to her?"

A warm feeling settled inside my chest at the thought of Mia. "Mia is my girlfriend."

Cooper's expression was unreadable, and Captain Rucker maintained his stern expression, as if nothing pleased him. I hoped I wouldn't say the wrong things, but my only choice was to tell the truth as I knew it.

"Ethan, can you tell me how you came to know Mia and when you learned of DFOG?"

"Well, actually, it was my pet wolves that found Mia."

Captain Rucker's eyebrows shot up, but he quickly wiped the astonishment off his face. I understood his surprise. It's not every day that you hear that someone has wolves for pets.

"My grandma and I were taking my wolves for a walk when they caught the scent of something and pulled us in its direction, leading us to a cave where we found Mia. She was pretty messed up and unconscious. We brought her back to my grandma's clinic, where my grandma treated her."

Switching topics, I addressed her question about DFOG. "Mia didn't immediately tell me about DFOG. I'm not sure if she would have ever mentioned it, but she and I were involved in an incident. Two guys, whom I knew from school, came after me, and Mia transformed into a wolf-like creature that I had never seen before, while the two guys ran away. Mia shifted to protect me." I paused to see if I should keep going or if they had any questions. Neither one said anything, just stared at me, so I continued. "The whole thing totally freaked me out, and I needed answers. She finally confessed about being homeless, her abduction, being handed over to the military, being experimented on, and being injected with something she didn't consent to. She also told me about my grandma being listed as an emergency contact for a DFOG member and her escaping from DFOG.

"At that point, we went to my grandma, and she contacted Sheriff Reid. He reached out to his FBI contact, who in turn contacted BSI. That's when you and Gibson became involved. You know the rest."

Agent Cooper glanced at something on the wall behind me and then fixed her gaze on me. "Thank you, Ethan. For the record, when you say Mia changed during the incident, can you describe exactly what you saw?"

I nodded, my throat suddenly dry. "When the guys cornered us, Mia changed. She kind of growled, and her eyes turned bright gold. She grew fangs, and these sharp claws sprang from her fingernails. She was also incredibly strong. I'd had a really bad asthma attack, and she picked me up and put me in my Jeep like I weighed nothing."

Captain Rucker watched me closely but said nothing.

Cooper kept her eyes on me and continued. "Did Mia ever explain DFOG's purpose in creating these hybrids?"

I hesitated before confirming. "She said DFOG wanted to create super soldiers. She and thirty-seven others were their test subjects, but six individuals died during the experiments. She said that the DNA injections enhanced their abilities, transforming powerful hybrids with amplified senses, but you know all this."

Cooper was quiet for a moment, her gaze distant. "And these soldiers, they can control these abilities?"

"Yes. I've seen Mia turn it on and off several times."

"Is there anything else you think we should know?"

I shook my head.

"Thank you, Ethan. Your statement is on record. I'll take you to the waiting area where your grandmother is already waiting."

"And Mia?" I asked.

"Her interview is still in progress."

Still in progress? For how long? I hoped she was okay. I needed to see her, but it seemed I had no choice but to wait. At least my grandma would be with me.

Cooper led me back down the hallway into an open area filled with chairs and tables, where, again, there was a coffee station and bottled water on the counter, but no refrigerator or sodas. My grandma was sitting in one of the seats facing the hallway. She smiled as our eyes met, and she waved me over.

"Thank you, Ethan," Cooper said again, and then turned around and headed back into the hallway.

Perhaps she went to discuss what I had said with Captain Rucker. But who knows? I'm sure I'd never find out, but I could find out what happened with my grandma's interview. Taking a seat next to her, I immediately asked, "How did your interview go? What did they ask you? Do you know when Mia's started?"

She raised her brows at me and tilted her head to the side. "We went into rooms at the same time, but I don't know when hers started. We probably shouldn't discuss our interviews, but I know how you are, Ethan, so I'll say this. Mine was straightforward, and the conversation was centered on your father."

"You mean that I'm persistent and don't let things go?"

"That's exactly what I mean."

Grumbling, I flopped back down in the chair. "I just want me and Mia to get back to having normal lives." I glanced at her and sarcastically added, "Again, something I can thank my parents for."

She bobbed her chin in understanding, then asked, "What does Mia want?"

I turned sharply to face her. What did she mean by that? Was she implying that Mia couldn't lead a normal life because of who she was, or was she suggesting that Mia didn't want a life with me?

"What I mean is that Mia is different from you and me," Grandma emphasized. "A normal life might be difficult for her. She cares for you deeply, Ethan, and that's evident in everything she does. But you need to try to see things from her perspective."

"I didn't know I wasn't already doing that?"

Grandma's expression softened as she placed her hand on my knee. "Then, just keep doing what you're doing."

"Can I ask you something? Well, it's really more that I need your approval."

"Go ahead."

"Um," I pursed my lips and frowned before blurting out, "I want to ask Mia to move in with me at our house. You're not her doctor anymore, so it wouldn't be unethical or anything."

She had that look—advice was coming. "You and Mia are both so young. My suggestion would be to wait. Spend some more time dating before taking this step."

"Really, Grandma? Is that what you and Grandpa did? Weren't you both younger than Mia and me?"

She chuckled. "You're absolutely right. When you know, you know." She smiled warmly at me. "You have my approval, Ethan."

I leaned over to hug her. "Thank you, Grandma. I'm excited to ask Mia. I wonder how much longer her interview will be. What can they be asking her that's taking so long?"

"You and I only just became aware of DFOG, and we only knew a small portion of what they were doing. Mia spent eleven years there. The agents probably have many questions for her." A frown creased her forehead. "I am concerned about her surgical sites. Sitting upright for this long is probably putting a strain on her incisions. I did bring her pain medication with me just to be on the safe side."

"She was already in pain during the drive over here," I confirmed, "but she was annoyed with me for worrying about her. Maybe you could speak with her once she's out of the interview room and encourage her to take the pain medication."

Before she could respond, the sound of approaching footsteps came from the hallway. Instantly, I was up on my feet, eyeing the entrance to the waiting area. Gibson and Cooper stood on either side of Mia as they stepped through the doorway. Mia's complexion was almost as white as the walls behind her, and I could see the tightness around her eyes. She held herself stiffly, and her steps seemed uneven. One arm was pressed protectively over her abdomen, and she was favoring her left leg.

Gibson politely nodded in our direction, and Cooper led Mia over to where we were standing. I noticed how Mia hesitated with every step.

My grandma put her arm around Mia. "Oh, sweetheart—" she started, her voice edged with worry.

Mia flashed a quick, brittle smile. "I'm fine, really." Her words sounded more like a reflex than the truth.

I exchanged a look with Grandma and saw her concern reflected back at me. Mia's shoulders were hunched, and she was breathing quickly. The pain Mia showed during the drive over, combined with her current state and Grandma's comments about the surgical sites, made it clear that she was in a lot of pain.

Cooper seemed to notice something was wrong, too, as she kept staring at Mia. Finally, she said, "Thank you all for your cooperation and providing such detailed information. We'll follow up if we need anything else. An agent will drive you back to your hotel."

"I think we need to wait a bit," Grandma said, studying Mia, who was wincing and holding her side. "Ethan, can you pull two chairs together so Mia can lie back and rest?"

Cooper stepped in and helped me quickly pull chairs together, turning them to face each other so Mia could stretch out. It wasn't perfect, but it made a kind of makeshift chaise that looked a lot more comfortable than sitting upright. My grandma and Gibson gently guided Mia down, helping her ease back and settle in without putting any strain on her abdomen or her leg.

"Let's get you comfortable, honey," Grandma said, already reaching into her bag for the pain medication. "Ethan, can you get some water?"

"Yeah, sure." I hurried over to the coffee station in the corner, grabbed bottled water, and rushed back, unscrewing the cap as I handed it to Grandma.

Grandma pressed a pain pill into Mia's palm and the bottled water in the other. "Take this, dear. It'll help."

She took it with a quiet "Thanks," her hand shaking just a little. Mia swallowed the pill with a sip of water, then leaned back and closed her eyes.

My grandma turned to Gibson and Cooper. "Can you come back and check on us in about fifteen minutes? I think the medicine will have taken effect by then. We can determine then if we're ready to be driven back to the hotel."

"Of course," Cooper agreed. "Is there anything else we can get you?"

"The medication should be enough, thank you."

Cooper nodded, and she and Gibson left the waiting area.

Grandma and I sat with Mia for about fifteen minutes, letting the medication take effect. The room was quiet except for the distant sounds of voices in the hallway. Eventually, some of the tension eased from Mia's face, and her breathing slowed to a relaxed rhythm.

A few minutes later, Cooper returned and asked, "How is she doing?"

"Her pain has subsided," Grandma said. "I think we're ready for that ride now."

***

Back in the hotel, my grandma helped Mia change into PJs, and then together, we got Mia into bed. My grandma ordered some chicken noodle soup from the room service for Mia and pasta for her and me.

I placed a TV tray over Mia's lap. She was clearly drowsy from the pain medication, so I took it upon myself to feed her the soup. She managed to eat half the bowl along with a few crackers, took a few sips of water, and then pushed the tray away. I set the tray on the dresser and then helped her lie down, fluffed her pillows, and pulled the blankets over her. I laid down next to her and gently stroked her hair. She gazed at me with heavy, tired eyes, smiled, and whispered, "I love you, Ethan," before closing her eyes and drifting off into a drugged sleep.

My heartbeat soared inside me as her words pierced my soul. For a moment, I just stared at her, hardly daring to breathe, replaying her words in my head. Warmth swelled in my chest, something fierce and gentle all at once. I brushed a stray lock of hair off her face and whispered, "I love you too, Mia," even though I knew she couldn't hear me. In utter bliss, I watched her sleep as I lay beside her, holding her hand.

CHAPTER 13

I woke up early, showered, and quietly slipped out of the bedroom to avoid waking Mia. My grandma's bedroom door was closed, so I assumed she was still asleep. I logged onto the hotel's laptop and ordered breakfast for everyone: scrambled eggs, bacon, sourdough toast, and fresh fruit. In the kitchen, I began brewing a pot of coffee. Rich, dark roast wafted under my nose.

I heard a door creak, and then my grandma came into the kitchen in her pajamas, robe, and slippers. "The coffee smells wonderful," she said, grabbing a mug and pouring herself a cup.

"I ordered breakfast, too."

She patted my shoulder. "You're a wonderful grandson."

I flashed a wide grin. "I try."

A knock at the door interrupted us, and I jogged over to answer, ready to dive into some scrambled eggs. Pulling the door open, I found Gibson and Cooper standing there. My shoulders slumped, and I had to swallow the disappointing sigh rising in my throat. "Now what?" popped into my head, but I did the polite thing and allowed them to come inside. "Morning," I said.

"Good morning, Ethan. Please excuse the early hour and the unexpected visit, but we thought you all would want to hear the news."

Grandma came into the sitting area with her coffee. "What news?" She waved her free hand in an apologetic gesture. "I'm sorry. Good morning."

Gibson shook off. "No worries." He glanced around the room. "Can Mia join us?"

"She's still sleeping," I said. "Yesterday was hard on her."

"I'm up," Mia said, coming up behind me.

I tucked my arm around her waist, her words from last night resurfacing and swirling in my head. I pushed aside the joyful buzz and centered on the agents. Another knock at the door came, and I left Mia's side to answer it. This time it was our breakfast, and I had room service set everything up on the table and gave them a tip before they left.

Cooper glanced at our food on the table. "I'm sorry. I promise this conversation won't take long, and then we'll be out of your way."

Gibson nodded in agreement. "I apologize as well. We should have called first, but we had to deliver this news in person. We received a call from General McClain regarding decommissioning of the DFOG department, and a plea deal was negotiated with the U.S. Attorney's office. The DOJ has accepted the deal. There will be no trial and no disruption to your lives."

"What?" I exclaimed, crossing my arms in a huff. "They're not going to fight? They're quitting before they even start?"

"There was a lot of evidence and many witness statements; a plea bargain was recommended."

"They'd better be facing some serious jail time."

"Ethan," Grandma interjected, her voice rising in surprise.

I glanced at her, realizing she might have a point, but I didn't care. Everyone involved in that mess needed to be held accountable.

Gibson's jaw tightened, seemingly surprised by the plea deal as well. "No one is getting off easy. These were serious federal charges, and as part of the deal, they all pled guilty." He glanced briefly at me. "This includes your parents, Ethan. What the deal secured for them was that the death penalty was taken off the table. They'll be serving life in federal prison with no possibility of parole."

Mia's eyes grew large as she asked, "They're going to prison? All of them?"

He nodded firmly. "Justice has been served, Mia."

"I can't believe it's over," Mia shook her head, "just like that."

"I wish we could have stopped them sooner," Cooper said, "but because of you, Mia, and you, Ethan, we were able to end this nightmare." She looked at Gibson and gestured toward the door. "We'll get going and let you enjoy your meal."

My grandma walked with them to the door. "Thank you, and I don't say that lightly, being Garrison's mother, but you saved many lives, and for that I'm grateful."

Gibson shook my grandma's hand. "It's our job, Dr. Porter. No need to thank us."

With that, they walked out of our hotel room. We stood motionless for a minute or two, and then slowly we gravitated toward the table and sat down and began to eat.

"How are you feeling about what's happening to Dad, Grandma?" I really could care less about either of my parents. They deserved punishment for what they did, but my dad was my grandma's son. I couldn't imagine what a parent would feel like if their child was guilty of a crime and went to prison. It had to be a horrible feeling, and while I didn't care about them, I loved my grandma and didn't want to see her hurt.

Her fork full of eggs paused in midair as she considered my question. She laid her fork down and said, "I feel a bit betrayed that he lied to me, to us, for so long, and I'm hurt and shocked at the same time. It's difficult to believe he chose to manipulate people's lives in such a horrifying way. It's going to be a very long time before I forgive my son." She looked at Mia. "I know I've said I'm sorry, but it just doesn't feel like it's enough."

Mia took my grandma's hand and softly said, "Evelyn, when I came across your name, I had no doubts that it would be you who helped me." Mia glanced at me and smiled. "At that time, I didn't know about Ethan, but he has been a light in all this darkness." She squeezed my grandma's hand. "You saved my life, and I am so grateful that I came into yours."

Tears glistened in my grandma's eyes, clearly touched by Mia's words, and she reached across the table to hug Mia. For several seconds they held each other before pulling away.

Once more, there was a knock at the hotel door. I sighed. "I'll get it. Geez, it's like Grand Central Station in here!"

When I opened the door, I found Briggs and Locke standing there. My gut reaction was to shut the door. I mean, what was this BSI intrusion day? Instead, I was polite. "Hey," I said, stepping aside and letting them enter.

"Well, hello," Grandma said. "Would either of you like a cup of coffee?"

Briggs waved away her offer. "No, thanks, Dr. Porter. Actually, we're here to speak to Mia." He looked at Mia. "Would that be okay, Mia?"

Mia sat down on the sofa, her eyes fixed on the two agents. "I guess so."

I furrowed my brows, studying them as I wondered, "What could they possibly want to discuss with Mia?"

My grandma's expression briefly mirrored mine before she nodded. "All right, I'll leave you to talk."

I hesitated, unsure if I should leave as well. I took a step back from Mia, but she reached out for my hand.

"Can you please stay, Ethan?"

"Of course." I sat down next to her, and I, too, stared at them, waiting.

Briggs and Locke remained standing, and it was Briggs who spoke first. "Mia, you know we've witnessed your abilities firsthand. You weren't just following orders from Gibson and Cooper. You were trying to save lives. That didn't go unnoticed."

Locke nodded. "We've both seen what you're capable of under pressure. Not just as a super soldier, but as someone who thinks fast and cares about the people around her. That's exactly what we need at BSI."

Mia cocked her head, eyeing them. "What are you saying?"

Briggs's mouth quirked into a half-smile. "We're offering you a place at BSI. Of course, there's a process—protocols, training, evaluations. You'd have to go through all of it, just like anyone else. Your unique skill set and what we've seen from you make us want to sponsor you. You'd have our backing, and we'd be your supervisory special agents."

Locke added, "You'd be starting as a new agent trainee and be assigned to a squad under either me or Briggs. There's also a ton of paperwork, background checks, and a whole lot of other crap you'll need to go through, but based on your performance during DFOG, we believe you're more than capable."

Mia glanced at me again, uncertainty in her eyes. I nodded, giving her a small, encouraging smile.

Briggs continued, "You've already proven yourself in ways most never get the chance to. What you did during the DFOG operation wasn't just impressive; it was inspiring. That's why we want you to join BSI."

"What about the other super soldiers?" Mia asked. "What's happening to them?"

"Social services has stepped in," Briggs explained. "They're working with each of them, finding them safe housing and jobs, and providing counseling for the trauma they went through and to help them re-enter normal life."

"Yeah, they're getting the full treatment," Locke chimed in. "You know, all the fun stuff that comes after surviving a covert nightmare. The goal is to make sure they can live like regular people and not, you know, vigilantes or hermits in the woods. We'll be checking in on them, just in case anyone gets the urge to do anything dramatic."

Mia breathed a sigh of relief. "We all deserve a normal life. I'm glad they're getting help."

Locke shrugged, the hint of a smirk tugging at his mouth. "As normal as anyone can be after that whole chaotic mess."

Briggs shot Locke a look but said nothing. Instead, he turned back to Mia. "We know it might be a challenging time for the soldiers, but we'll do right by them. Just like we want to do right by you."

Mia sat quietly for a moment, her gaze distant, fingers tightening around mine. She looked at Briggs and Locke, her lips parting as if she was about to answer. From the determined set of her jaw and the uncertainty in her eyes, I was certain she was going to refuse.

Before she could speak, Briggs gently raised a hand. "You don't have to answer now, Mia. Think about it. Take the time you need and let us know when you're ready. Whatever your decision is, we'll support it."

Sincerity softened Locke's usual sarcasm as he said, "We'll be around. Just send up a signal when you're ready to talk."

Briggs had that kind smile plastered onto his face as he said, "We'll wait to hear from you."

With that, Briggs and Locke made their way to the door. They paused to nod politely to my grandma, who'd peeked out from the kitchen. The door clicked softly shut behind them, leaving Mia with an important decision to make.

"What are you thinking, Mia?" My pulse quickened as nerves took over. Inwardly, I pleaded that her answer be no. I couldn't lose her, especially when I was just about to ask her to move in with me.

She turned toward me, a beautiful smile spreading on her face. "My soldier days are over. Besides, there's this adorable guy in Doford Peaks who I've had my eye on."

My grandma chuckled and disappeared back into the kitchen.

Laughter burst out of me before I could contain my delight, and I hoped I didn't look like a fool. I inhaled a breath and blew it out, clearing my head and then planted a big kiss on her lips. "I was really hoping you'd say that." I pulled away quickly and added, "Not about the adorable guy thing, but about not being a soldier."

She giggled, her eyes sparkling with bliss. "I knew what you meant, silly." Then she kissed me, soft and tender, making my heart race even faster.

This was my moment to tell Mia. I felt a rush of emotion building inside me. I looked her in the eyes and said, "Mia, move in with me at my grandma's house. I want to be with you every single day."

Her smile grew brighter, if that was possible. "Yes!" she blurted out and threw her arms around me.

CHAPTER 14

We arrived in Doford Peaks the next day, late in the afternoon. While my grandma went to check on her clinic, Mia and I climbed into my Jeep and drove over to Sarah and Glen's house to pick up Hank and Gracie, as well as to pack Mia's belongings.

Hank's and Gracie's howls met my ears before the door even opened. Sarah barely managed to step aside as they barreled through the front door, howling and whining while jumping all over Mia and me. We both lost our balance and ended up sitting on the porch, surrendering to their enthusiastic licks. Though, I didn't mind. I'd missed my wolves and was overjoyed to see them and hear how excited they were to have us back home.

Scratching their ears, I said, "We missed you, too!"

Mia was smothering Hank and Gracie with kisses and hugs.

"They certainly missed you both," Sarah said. "How are you both doing? I know you've been through an ordeal, to say the least."

I put my arm around Mia. "It's been challenging, especially with Mia being injured."

Sarah rested her hand on Mia's forearm. "How are you, dear?"

"I'm okay. Every day gets a little better. Thank you for asking."

"Of course."

"And thank you so much for taking excellent care of Hank and Gracie, Sarah," I added. "I really appreciated that, as we were going through a lot, and that was one less thing off my mind."

"You're very welcome. They were both absolute dreams to take care of." She waved us forward. "Come inside. Even though spring is upon us, there's still a chill in the air."

Mia and I followed Sarah inside, and Hank and Gracie trotted happily beside us.

"Let me gather Hank's and Gracie's toys and food. Evelyn brought everything over in a large container, so I'll pack it up for you."

"Actually, Sarah, can you wait just a minute?" Mia asked.

Sarah stopped, an expression of concern coming over her.

Mia waved her hand in an apologetic gesture. "Nothing's wrong. I just wanted to let you know that I don't need the rental anymore because I'm moving in with Ethan."

A smile spread on her face. "I'm not surprised. In fact, a couple of weeks ago, I told Glen he'd better start looking for a new tenant. I'm happy for you both, and the fact that you're so close means we can visit anytime."

"Thank you, Sarah, and Glen, too. You've both done so much for Mia and me."

"Yes, thank you both," Mia echoed.

"You don't need to thank me. That's what friends are for. Let me get Hank's and Gracie's things. Oh, did you bring boxes for Mia's things?"

"We have a few duffel bags in my Jeep since it's just clothes, shoes, and a few other personal items," I said. "Thank you, though. Do you need help with getting Hank's and Gracie's stuff?"

Sarah waved me off and left us to gather their belongings. Hank and Gracie stayed close to us, but they were much calmer and no longer howling and whining.

"I can't believe we're back home, and soon we'll be back to doing normal stuff, and I'll be scooping ice cream at The Ice House?"

"I can always go for free ice cream."

She giggled and nudged me. "You and your ice cream."

"What? It's super good, and even better when it's free."

Mia kissed my cheek. "For you, always."

When Sarah returned with the container, I rushed over to take it from her. Mia hugged Sarah tightly for a good minute, asking, "Do you want to come with me while I get my keys?"

Sarah shook her head. "Just leave the key on the kitchen counter. I'll come by later to pick it up. You two take all the time you need to pack."

"Thank you again, Sarah. Please tell Glen thank you as well."

"Will do. Tell Evelyn I said hello."

"I will."

Mia, Hank, Gracie, and I walked out of the house and over to my Jeep. I put my wolves' container in the back and grabbed the duffle bags for Mia's things. I glanced at Mia. "Are you ready?"

"So ready. You?"

"Yep. Let's do this."

Holding hands, we walked over to the rental, opened the door, and Hank and Gracie ran in first. We stepped inside, the place already feeling half-forgotten. Hank and Gracie explored the space, their noses twitching with curiosity. Mia tossed a duffle bag on the bed and glanced at me. "It won't take long. Just my clothes, shoes, and bathroom stuff. I didn't really have a chance to collect anything, and the furniture is theirs, so..."

"Okay." I picked up a bag. "Want me to start in the closet?"

Mia nodded. "Yeah, thanks. I'll get the bathroom." Hank followed close behind her, his tail wagging.

Sliding open the closet door, I peered inside. A few hangers held a rotation of joggers, hoodies, T-shirts, jeans, and a couple of sweaters. Two pairs of sneakers and a pair of boots lay on the floor. Pulling her clothes off the hangers and folding them, I laid the soft, familiar fabrics in the duffle bag. It struck me how little there was. Gracie watched me from the doorway, ears perked. When the closet was empty, I moved to the dresser, opening the top drawers. Neatly folded inside were Mia's underwear and bras. Trying to be respectful, I quickly tucked them into the bag.

From the bathroom, the faint clatter of bottles spilled into the bedroom. Hank's paws clicked softly on the tile as he supervised whatever
was going on there.

I called out, "I think I'm done. Unless there's more somewhere else?"

Mia appeared in the doorway, the bag in her hand, and shrugged.
"That's it. There wasn't much to begin with."

I zipped up the bags, feeling the weight—or rather, the lightness—of
her life. Mia's eyes met mine, and a light of hope filled them. Hank nudged
Mia's hand, and Gracie circled back to stand at her side. Mia patted both
their heads.

I slung the two duffle bags over my shoulder. "Ready?"

She smiled. "Ready."

With Hank and Gracie leading the way, we stepped out of the
rental—everything Mia owned packed into just two bags. I loaded them
into the back of my jeep, and Mia settled into the passenger seat while
Hank and Gracie hopped easily into the back seat, tails thumping against
the leather. I hopped into the driver's seat, started the engine, and
glanced at Mia, who reached over and squeezed my hand.

"Let's go home," she said, her face beaming.

With the wolves peering out the windows and the late afternoon sun
filtering through the trees, we pulled away from the curb, leaving the
rental behind and heading together, all four of us, toward Grandma's
house and our new beginning just ten minutes down the road.

"Everything has changed," Mia said, her breath shaky.

I swallowed the concern rising in my throat. "Is that okay?"

"Everything is fine. It's just that I can't believe how my life has evolved."

"But it's for the better," I reassured her.

"And we have each other."

I leaned over and kissed her cheek, my eyes still focused on the road.
"Yes, and now we get to share every day together."

"That's the best part."

As I turned onto our street, an incredible warmth filled me. I was
bringing the girl I loved home. All the craziness was behind us, and we

were free to live our lives as ordinary people. Which, in a way, was a little bit amusing; a boy with asthma and a wolf-human hybrid girl were going to live normal lives.

"What are you thinking?" Mia asked.

"Nothing," I said. "I'm just happy."

"Me too."

"We're here," I said, pulling into the driveway and then clicking the remote to enter the garage.

I grabbed the container and a duffle bag, while Mia took the other one. As I opened the door to the house, Hank and Gracie dashed inside, eagerly searching for my grandma. I heard her voice coming from the living room. "Hank, Gracie, I missed you!" Their excited whines filled the air.

We headed into the living room and then set our things on the floor. Hank and Gracie were sitting on either side of Grandma on the couch, with their noses pressed against her face. My grandma's gaze shifted to the bags, and then she looked at me. I spread a big smile on my face. Rising from the sofa, Grandma walked over and took Mia's hands in hers. "I'm happy to welcome you into our home, dear. While you settle in and unpack your things, I'll whip up a delicious dinner to celebrate."

"Thank you, Evelyn."

"You don't have to thank me, dear. Go unpack and then relax. I'll let you know when dinner's ready." My grandma smiled and patted Mia's hand before leaving and going to make dinner, with Hank and Gracie following, probably hoping for some treats.

I left the container in the living room, grabbed Mia's bags, and then took her hand and brought her to my room. I set her bags on my bed and cleared out one of my dresser drawers, some space in the closet, and another drawer in the bathroom. "Is this enough space, Mia? If not, I can make more room."

Unpacking and putting her things away, she said, "It's plenty." She winked at me. "For now."

"I take it that means you plan to buy more stuff."

"You guessed right."

I kissed her, then said, "I'll invest in that."

"Aw, that's so sweet."

"I try," I teased. "While we wait for dinner, do you want to sit on the back deck and watch the sunset?"

"Yes, I'd love that."

I took her hand and led her into the kitchen. Grandma was chopping peppers on the counter, and Hank and Gracie were lying at her feet. I inhaled deeply as the spicy scent of Mexican flavors filled the kitchen. "It smells wonderful, Grandma. Mia and I are going outside until dinner's ready. Unless you need us to help with anything."

She waved us off. "Go relax, I've got this."

I slid the glass door open and took Mia out onto the wooden deck. The smell of pine and burning wood replaced the Mexican scents. I led her toward the lounge chairs surrounding the firepit, where the flames crackled, sending sparks flying and vanishing into the sky, which was streaked with ribbons of pinks, purples, and oranges. We sat down in two cushioned lounge chairs facing the mountains. The sun had just begun to set, its golden hue blending into the trees.

I glanced at Mia, catching the reflection of the changing sky in her eyes. Her presence captivated me, and I couldn't contain the smile from spreading on my face.

She glanced over at me, her cheeks glowing with a rosy pink. "I heard you, you know."

I squished my brows together. "What do you mean?"

She smiled that beautiful smile of hers. "After I told you that I loved you, I heard you say it back."

I pressed my hand over my heart as I said, "I do love you, Mia."

Her eyes glistened with tears. "And I love you, Ethan."

I rose from my chair and joined her in hers, wrapping my arm around her. She snuggled up against me and rested her head on my shoulder. Together, we watched the sun drift below the mountains, and the last rays of sunlight vanished across the wooden deck. A deep blue enveloped the sky above us, signaling the arrival of night. Mia's heart beat against mine, and in that perfect moment, there was only us.

Even in the dim light, her eyes sparkled as she looked up at me. "Whatever tomorrow brings, we'll face it together, right?"

I squeezed her hand. "Always."

As the first stars blinked into the velvet sky, I knew with absolute certainty that I belonged here. With her. With hope. With love.

Epilogue

That's the story of how I met my wife seven years ago. In one way, my parents were right: I don't suffer from asthma anymore. But it wasn't just time that healed me. I breathe easier now because of Mia's love and support, the joy of raising our daughters—Jade, who is six, and Emma, who is five—and letting go of the resentment toward my parents have all played their part.

Those seven years have transformed us all. Grandma retired and started dating Sheriff Reid, her eyes twinkling with this new adventure. Hank and Gracie, our wolves, are still full of energy at eight, always by Emma's side, who continues to surprise us. When Emma turned three, we noticed her eyes shifting between turquoise and gold. Grandma ran tests and found that Emma had Mia's genes and Jade had mine; it all clicked, and the miracle of Emma is a reminder of the magic in our lives. Jade is like me, gentle and thoughtful, happiest with a book or a puzzle, while Emma is like Mia, bold and adventurous, often racing through the mountain paths with Hank and Gracie at her heels. Jade's calm personality often keeps Emma's wild side in check. Even though they are different, they are still very close. They care for each other, and every day they remind us of ourselves.

Mia and I became entrepreneurs and took a chance and purchased The Ice House. It's been a wild adventure for Mia and me, dreaming up new flavors. Some were hits and some definite misses. We spent many late nights brainstorming and reimagining in The Ice House kitchen while Grandma watched the girls, whom she spoils every chance she gets.

Locke and Briggs have never really left our lives, even if miles and years stretch between us. Every so often, they reach out to Mia for her expertise—strange cases that defy explanation or supernatural mysteries. Thankfully, technology kept Mia safe at home, reviewing their findings online while I sat beside her, grateful that her brilliance could shine from the safety of our den.

When we told Grandma we wanted to buy a house, she was beside herself and insisted that if we had to move, we would build on her land. In the end, Grandma won, and we're one big happy family sharing holidays, dinners, and daily life just a short walk apart. It's chaotic at times, but it's ours.

Looking back, I never dreamed that any of those experiences would be my life. I was just a young man struggling to breathe, unsure of my place in the world. Now, I'm surrounded by family, love, and the kind of everyday miracles I once thought were out of reach. No matter what you're going through, never give up hope. That's what I've learned. Keep your faith strong and never stop believing. Happiness has a way of finding you, sometimes in the most unexpected forms. Miracles happen. You simply need to be open to recognizing them when they come.

About the Author

LAURA DALEO is an accomplished multi-genre author known for weaving captivating tales across dark fantasy, urban fantasy, supernatural/paranormal, sci-fi, and young adult fiction. Her acclaimed Immortal Kiss series showcases her unique take on vampiric lore, reimagining the origins of vampires through the lens of the Egyptian pantheon. Originally from San Diego, California, Laura now calls Tucson, Arizona home, where she shares her life with her two beloved dogs, Rose and Cooper.